THE ALIBI

BY

KELLY KEY

Kelly Key

ISBN: 979-8-218-89867-0 (Paperback)

Library of Congress Control Number: 00000000000

Any references to historical events, real people, or real places are used fictitiously. Names, characters, and places are products of the author's imagination.

Edited by Lesley Key, Antioch, Tennessee.

Front cover image by Kelly Key.

Book cover design by Rosey Moehle, Franklin, Tennessee.

Printed in the United States of America.

COZY/CONCE PUBLISHING

715 Key Road

Lafayette, Tennessee 37083

All of Kelly Key's books can be found on Amazon.com and at:

https://kellykeybooks.com/

The Alibi

DEDICATION

This book is dedicated to the muse who visited me one night and planted this story in my head. Hey, don't be a stranger! Visit anytime you want!

TABLE OF CONTENTS

CHAPTER 1 1

CHAPTER 2 11

CHAPTER 3 25

CHAPTER 4 37

CHAPTER 5 51

CHAPTER 6 63

CHAPTER 7 77

CHAPTER 8 89

CHAPTER 9 101

CHAPTER 10 115

CHAPTER 11 127

CHAPTER 12 139

CHAPTER 13 153

CHAPTER 14 167

Kelly Key

CHAPTER 15 181

CHAPTER 16 193

CHAPTER 17 205

CHAPTER 18 217

ABOUT THE AUTHOR 229

CHAPTER 1

Leaning against the doorway of her room, Eloise looked her client up and down, assessing him. In the hallway in front of Eloise's door, stood a thin, frail-looking man with slicked-back hair of about 40 years of age, at her estimate. She finished her appraisal of the man before her and thought, "This shouldn't take long."

She managed a smile and purred, "Hey, Sugar. Did Carlos send you to see me?"

The little man shyly smiled and replied, "Yes. Yes, he did."

"Well, don't stand there all night, Sugar. We got things to do. Time is money, you know." She pulled back the door and waved her arm to invite him into the room.

"You got a name, Honey?" asked Eloise.

"William," he replied softly. "My name is William."

"Well, Billy Boy, what's your pleasure?"

"Don't call me that. My name is William," he said curtly.

Eloise threw up her hands defensively. "Sorry, William. I don't want to get off on the wrong foot. We're here to have fun. Now, what kind of fun do you want to have?"

"I want to hold your hands," said William.

Eloise cocked her head to the side in her confusion and said, "Okay, that's a slow start. Remember, William, you paid for an hour, then you gotta go. So, you might want to be more…in a hurry."

"Just the hands…please," William said as he tried to come down from the flash of anger over his name.

Eloise gave in. "You're the boss…" she acquiesced, giving her "John" her hands.

William took her hands in his and began caressing her palms and wrists. He lifted his gaze from her hands to meet Eloise's eyes.

"Such lovely hands," commented William, as he continued rubbing the hands, intertwining his fingers with hers.

"Um, thank you, William," said a confused Eloise. *Where is this going?* she wondered.

"Such loveliness in the world," said William, rubbing her fingers more roughly now. "It's a shame they'll have to go."

William suddenly lunged at Eloise's wrists. He pulled both to his right hand as Eloise was surprised by the sudden attack.

"What?" shrieked Eloise. She tried with all her strength to draw her hands away from William's surprisingly powerful grip.

"The hands are the first to go," William said determinedly. Keeping Eloise's hands in his right hand, he lifted his left to clamp around her mouth. Eloise started screaming and writhing to get away. But William's hold was too strong. He pushed her toward her bed.

"If I take the hands first, then you can watch, too. Well...for a little while..." William said in a calm, dead voice in a matter-of-fact tone, like he was going through the motions he'd done so many times, it was routine to him.

He pushed Eloise down on the bed and flipped her onto her stomach. The attacker reached for a pillow and stripped off the pillowcase. He then used it to gag Eloise as she continued to struggle to get away. He then pulled off his belt and wrapped it around her torso, pinning her arms to her sides.

Eloise screamed and screamed for help. But the gag did its job, muffling her calls. She wiggled and kicked, but to no avail. She was his prisoner.

William flipped her over, so she was face-up. He placed his knee on her chest to keep her from struggling. Once satisfied that she could not move anymore, William reached around and retrieved a rectangular leather case from his back pocket. He popped the latch on the side and pulled out a long scalpel. Dropping the leather case beside Eloise, he ran his finger up and down the instrument, almost caressing it. He smiled as he looked at his victim.

"Now, Eloise, don't protest. Don't try to get away. Just sit back and enjoy the show…"

With a stabbing thrust, William pushed the scalpel into the top of her right wrist and began to carve her hand away from her arm. The sound of tendons and gristles being sliced could still be heard over Eloise's muffled screams. With one more push, William severed her hand, lifted it from her bed, and shoved it toward her face. The blood from the opened end ran in a thin stream and spilled onto her shocked face. Her eyes grew wider with fear as the realization that she was going to die.

William smiled, breathing in the fear he was creating in her. He then proceeded to her left hand and severed it. Pools of Eloise's blood collected on the dirty sheets of her bed. William proceeded with his dismemberments. He turned to her blood-stained legs and feet, which had stopped kicking with the loss of her blood.

*

William Arbogast bolted awake in a cold sweat. He had fallen asleep at his kitchen table, too scared and not daring to go to bed. His chest heaving from panic, he looked down at his white, sweat-stained shirt to look for blood stains. There were none. He lifted his hands to examine them. Again, no stains or any other evidence of what he had just experienced was real. But it had to be. He felt Eloise. He smelled her perfume. He felt her skin. He felt her blood. He felt her struggle. He heard her screams. It had to be real. William knew that, somehow, he had been in this prostitute's room and dismembered her till she bled out.

William's panic overwhelmed him, and he jumped to his feet. He had to make this madness stop. He had to protect himself and more potential victims before he was overcome again. The slight man grabbed his black coat and ran out the door, not bothering to lock it after he slammed it shut.

*

Jack Banks rolled over in his bed. The spot next to him was empty but still warm. He rubbed it up and down with his left arm as if caressing the woman who had been lying there not too long ago. Jack broke a smile thinking of their exploits just a few hours ago. He told himself that he had married well. Clemmie was a young, intelligent woman with a good heart and was very good to him. He rolled over on his back and stared at the ceiling. He knew he had to rise for work. But he didn't want to leave this bed of contentment and pleasure.

Then Jack smelled bacon. Clemmie must have started breakfast on the gas range. Their apartment was relatively modern for 1910. It had gas hookups and electric lights, although the wiring was still being strung outside the walls. It was a comfortable little place, big enough for the two of them.

Jack rose and slipped on his pants. He went over to the water bowl, poured water from the pitcher, and splashed his face. He finished dressing and wandered into the kitchen, where he found his wife cooking their breakfast. Jack noticed she was wearing one of his shirts.

Her back was to him as she was busy rescuing the bacon from the hot skillet and placing the slices on a plate. Jack stealthily crept up behind Clemmie and wrapped his arms around her.

Clemmie jumped and let out a yelp. She had been concentrating on her cooking and the sizzling grease covered Jack's footsteps from being heard.

"Jack! You almost got a face full of grease. You should be more thoughtful around people with sharp objects!" she threatened, waving the long fork in her husband's face.

"Mornin'!" Jack responded. It was muffled as he buried his face in the nape of Clemmie's neck. "You didn't have to make me breakfast. I'm going to be late as it is."

"Who said I was making you anything to eat?" Clemmie asked sarcastically. "This bacon is mine!"

"Oh, come on, Clemmie!" Jack pleaded. "You were so giving last night. You gonna be selfish now?"

"I didn't oversleep," she said emphatically. "You did. Bacon's for early risers. Now, grab your coffee and git! I don't want the Chief knocking on our door looking for you," said Clemmie as she spun out of Jack's arms to head toward the kitchen table.

Jack reached for a potholder and poured some coffee from the pot sitting on the stove. He guzzled it from the big white cup as he walked hurriedly towards the kitchen table. Jack stood beside his wife and lifted her head to kiss her goodbye. Clemmie smiled and reciprocated with a long, passionate kiss. Jack used the opportunity that passion provided to grab a slice of bacon from Clemmie's plate and hurriedly chewed on it as he put his coat on.

"Thief!" accused Clemmie.

"I'm no thief!" pouted Jack, feigning hurt feelings. Then, he smiled and continued, "I catch them! Bye, Clem! Love you!"

∗

"Well now, if it ain't the late detective, Jack Banks!" Chief Dooley yelled at the precinct doors as Jack entered. He was trying to publicly shame his detective in front of the policemen on duty in the building.

"Sorry, Chief," Jack said contritely. He pulled off his coat as he walked toward his desk and hung it on the back of the chair. "No excuses, sir."

"I don't know why you even showed up at all," Dooley continued. "I would have waited till after lunch. It's so near time."

"Time got away from me, sir. It won't happen again," Jack said

"You hear that, Austin? It won't happen again..." chided the chief. "This wasn't a problem till you started shacking up with that woman."

"Clemmie had nothing to do with it," Jack defended his love. "I just overslept. Can we change the subject?"

"I'm going to have to meet this 'Clemmie' and give her a talking to. You're needed here, Detective Banks," Dooley said.

"So, I'm here!" Jack said with an impish smile. He saw that the chief wasn't charmed by his attitude. He let his face fall into seriousness and added, "What do you need, Chief?"

Satisfied he had scolded him enough, Dooley walked over to Jack's desk and placed a paper in front of the detective.

"I want you to interrogate this character. He came in all crazed last night, like he was on opium or something else wild. He claimed he cut up some whore, but he can't remember where it was. There's no blood on him. No torn clothes like someone resisted. We even checked his fingernails...all clean."

"So, what do you want me to do? Get him to admit it was a fever dream caused by whatever he took?" asked the detective.

"Here's the thing, Jack. There's been a rash of murders of women all over the city, above the norm. I'm sure this goon won't be the last disturbed person to admit to the killings once the newspapers get wind of it. By the looks of him, he wouldn't harm a fly. But if he did kill somebody, I'm not gonna be the District

Chief that had him and tossed him out without getting a statement. That's where you come in, Detective."

Jack looked down at the paper that his boss had given him. It read,

WILLIAM ARBOGAST

40 YEARS OLD

SINGLE

WHITE

ACCOUNTANT

"Arbogast's an accountant? That doesn't sound like the killing type," said Jack.

"It takes all kinds…" commented Chief Dooley. "See what you can find out."

"Don't you think my time would be better served than talking to some nutty man who wants to confess to crimes he didn't commit? You're doing this to punish me for being late, aren't you, Boss?" asked Jack.

"I'm giving it to you because everybody else here on this shift is already assigned for the day. You want a better case? Get here on time! The punishment is just icing on the cake. Now, go on. He's in the interrogation room," ordered the chief.

"Yes, sir," Jack answered sarcastically.

"Watch it, Detective. You're already in the doghouse. Don't shit where you sleep."

CHAPTER 2

William Arbogast sat alone in a black wooden chair. He rested his elbows on a black wooden table. He betrayed his anxiety by nervously wringing his shaking hands . It was apparent he was traumatized by what he'd witnessed himself doing the night before. Little droplets of sweat clung to his upper lip. With his head down, he pushed against his elbows to make his body rock back and forth slightly.

Detective Banks came through the door and slammed it behind him to reflect his frustration at being handed what he determined was a menial task. He took a breath to collect himself and calmed down. He knew he couldn't take out his frustrations on the meek-looking man before him. He took the seat across the table from William.

"Mister…" Jack started. He had to look down at the form before him to remember the name. "Arbogast. I'm Detective Jack Banks. Tell me, what brings you here?"

William cleared his throat and began, "It's right there on that paper you're reading. I killed a prostitute last night. I cut her up. I hacked off pieces of her till she died. Then I continued to dismember her corpse till only the torso remained."

"I see," said Jack. "What brought you to do such a thing?"

"That's just it. I don't know why. I couldn't stop myself. I had no control of my body. It was like my hands had a mind of their own, making me kill that poor woman, Eloise. I just kept cutting Eloise and hacking Eloise."

Saying Eloise's name rehumanized what had happened. William put his face in his hands and started sobbing in his guilt and shame for the murder.

"Eloise? That's mighty specific, William. Or should I call you Bill?" asked Jack.

"Call me William. No one calls me Bill," Arbogast corrected the detective as he sniffed and collected himself.

"That figures," Jack answered. Thinking to himself, the nervous man looked like a "William," not a "Bill."

"Where did this murder take place?" Jack asked.

"On the south side of town. I don't even know how I got there. I met Eloise at her door. I was directed to go to her room in a tenement building," William said, wiping his eyes and face with a handkerchief he had pulled out of his back pants pocket.

"The south side?" the detective asked. "That's all the way across town."

Jack looked down at the address William had written on the form and said, "It says here you live a few blocks away from this station. How did you get back up here if you killed 'Eloise' last night? Even the newfangled subway isn't that quick."

The unassuming man across the table from Jack tried to answer. But his bottom lip started to quiver, and he broke into another sob. "I don't know. I wish I could tell you. But I don't know. One minute, I'm standing over her body, and the next minute, I'm home. I don't know what's happening to me! I thought I was dreaming...like I have before. But I could feel her. I could taste her blood. I could feel the knife cutting through her body. The way she looked at me. And I couldn't stop. I just couldn't stop!"

William folded his arms on the table and buried his head in them. He released a mournful wail that could be heard all over the precinct hall. It made the officers in the building stop their paperwork and turn their heads toward the interrogation room.

Jack leaned back in his chair, letting William get it out of his system. He felt like he should be comforting the little man. He struggled to keep up his "detective persona." When William began to calm down, Jack rose and went to William. He placed his hand on William's shoulder.

"Do you think you can go back to the block where that building is? Can you show me?" the detective asked.

William thought for a minute, then nodded, saying, "If I saw it, I'd know it. Wait. There was a man. A man named Carlos. He sent me to Eloise."

"Listen, William," Jack began, "I have to step out a minute. If you need to take a break, you know, to go to the toilet or get a coffee, now would be a good time."

"I don't need or want anything. Except for protection. Protection from myself...if I can't control myself."

"Very well," said Jack. "I'll be back in a minute."

Jack left the room and went to the booking desk at the police station's entrance. Chief Dooley was standing at the desk, speaking with the booking officer. He looked to see Jack approach him.

"That was a quick interrogation, Detective," the chief said. "I can't believe you did a thorough job. Just what did you say to get him to howl like that?"

"I just came out to verify something," Jack answered. "Mr. Arbogast in there claims he hacked up a prostitute named...Eloise. Anybody reported in on something like that?"

"Whores get killed all of the time. Hell, it's practically an occupational hazard," said the chief.

The officer behind the desk laughed and commented, "Good one, Chief!"

"It's funny 'cause it's true, Austin," Dooley told the desk officer. "If a pimp did find one of his girls chopped up, he'd more than likely pick up the pieces, dump the body, and clean up the room for the next whore."

"Listen, Chief," said Jack. "Arbogast really believes he killed someone last night. He says he has no control over himself when he's doing the killing. He's scared to death he'll do it again. Here's the quandary: he says he did it on the city's south side. That's a speedy trip to get back up here by this morning."

"So, he's lying," concluded the chief.

"More than likely," Jack agreed. "He says he can take me to the tenement where she had a room. Suppose I take him down there, and when he can't find the building, he'll snap out of it, and problem solved."

"I didn't know you were such a do-gooder," chided Chief Dooley. "Why don't you call the Southern District station house and see if they know anything about a whore getting cut up last night. It'll save you a trip. I already know what they'll tell ya. I think Arbogast is daft."

"I was just about to do that, Chief," said Jack. "If there was a killing…"

"Then take your new friend to the Southern District station and have him confess to them. Then he's out of our hair. Problem solved," answered Dooley.

"That's why you're the chief!" Austin declared from behind the desk.

"Nobody likes an ass-kisser, Austin. Especially me!" the chief said. "Detective, make the call and get that guy out of here."

Jack reached across the front desk and grabbed the phone sitting in front of Officer Austin. He unhooked the earpiece and clicked the cradle a couple of times to get an operator on the line.

"Southern District Police Station, please," Jack said into the mouthpiece attached to the top of the phone. In 1910, phones had no dials. One had to speak to an operator to connect to the other line.

After a few clicks and rings, someone answered, "Southern District Station. Sergeant Petrillo speaking."

"Yes, Sergeant, this is Detective Banks from District Nine. We've got a guy who came in last night claiming to have murdered a prostitute on your side of town. Did you get any reports of a woman being hacked up last night?"

"Detective, you know you've called the Southern Precinct," the sergeant began. He didn't mean to talk down to a superior officer. But this wasn't the first time an officer called to inquire about the murder of a prostitute. "You can't swing a dead cat without hitting a dead prostitute in this part of town. We find them everywhere. You seriously think a pimp is going to run in here and report the murder of one of his girls? It is now twelve o'clock. By now, I'd say she's been sacked up and thrown in the river. So, to answer your question in a roundabout way, no Detective, no reports. And they'll probably never will be, rest her soul, if your guy did what he claims. In other words, in lawyer talk, corpus delicti. No body, no crime."

Jack sneered at the phone as if the officer on the other end could see him. Then he answered sarcastically, "Thanks, Petrillo. You've been very helpful."

"Anytime, Detective..." after they both hung up at the same time, Petrillo added, "Dick!"

*

The journey to the city's south side was as awkward as it was uneventful. The detective was following Chief Dooley's orders to escort the subject to the Southern Precinct and out of the chief's hair. Jack had sat beside William on the subway without a word spoken between them. To Jack, William seemed to be struggling internally with what had happened the previous night. The detective felt he could neither contribute nor aid the poor man's struggle. It did make the detective want to give him a shot to prove his story. The Southern District might have to wait a couple of hours.

"C'mon, Arbogast. We're getting off here," Jack said as he stood and pulled up William by the arm.

They emerged from the subway's exit to a busy street bustling with a mixture of early gas-powered vehicles, horse-drawn wagons, and buggies. Even this early in the afternoon, the sidewalks were heavy with pedestrians.

"Well, William, see anything that looks familiar? We don't have all day," said Jack, trying to light a fire under the lost man.

William looked around the cityscape in bewilderment. His eyes betrayed how lost he was to the detective. He finally shook his head in defeat.

"Look, the further south we go, the more whores we'll run up on. Maybe they can lead us to this Carlos guy," suggested Jack.

"Alright…" William agreed meekly.

They crossed the street, and the further south they walked, the more dilapidated the neighborhood became. Where suits and new hats were common on the people on the street, where they emerged from the subway, now dirty and ragged clothes were the norm. Jack felt for his pistol in his coat to ensure he had brought it.

It didn't take long for the pair to find a prostitute. Jack didn't have to use his detective skills in this part of town. A woman stopped them in the street and blatantly propositioned them.

"Good afternoon, gents!" said the woman. She wore what was simply a day dress. Its front buttons were undone to reveal her cleavage. She wanted it known that there were no undergarments to impede her work.

"You two look like you're looking for some fun," she continued. "You've found it. Fun's my middle name!" she said as she rubbed up against William.

William shyly recoiled and said, "No, thank you, ma'am. Good day!"

William started walking away, and Jack grabbed him by the shoulder. He pulled him back in front of the woman.

"Hang on, William," said Jack. "I think this is the kind of lady we're looking for."

"I'll be any kind of lady you want, sweetheart," she said, thinking she'd made a sale.

"Hang on," Jack interrupted her. "We're not looking for that. We're looking for a pimp. Name of Carlos."

The woman's head dropped. "I don't know anybody named Carlos. You looking to shake him down?"

Jack recognized the "tell" of her question. He said, "We're not here to make trouble, miss. We think one of his girls may be…in trouble."

"Oh yeah?" she said sarcastically. "And what's her name?"

"Eloise…" William uttered in a whisper.

A look of recognition and fear came over the prostitute's face. "Eloise? What kind of trouble are we talking about?"

"We'd rather not say," answered Jack. "We just want to make sure she's all right."

"Well, if I did know this Carlos, I wouldn't rat him out to the likes of you two," she said. "But if it's pimps you're looking for, I can tell you where they drink. But it'll cost you. You've already taken too much of my street time."

"How about two bucks?" asked Jack.

"Okay," she nodded. And added, "Two bucks will get you there."

"William, pay the woman," Jack ordered, as he tapped on the coat pocket where William would keep his wallet.

"Me?" protested William.

"You want to find this Carlos or not? Pay the woman so she can get back to work," Jack said with a threatening smile.

William looked around to see if anyone in this shady part of town was watching him. He reached into his coat and pulled his wallet from the pocket inside it. He handed the woman two silver dollars.

"Thanks, Love," the prostitute said as she tucked the money into the one pocket on her dress. "It's a place called Blackie's Bar. Go a couple of blocks down and turn right. You can't miss it."

"Thanks, ma'am. You've been very helpful," Jack said politely.

"Just one more thing, you didn't hear this from me," she added.

"We don't even know your name," Jack winked reassuringly at her.

"That wasn't by accident…" she murmured as she left them to find another "John."

*

The two made their way to Blackie's. Its entrance wasn't on the street. The bar's space was in a basement. When Jack and William entered, their eyes had to adjust from daylight to night. It was a dark place. Only lit by two lamps behind the bar and candles at the few tables in front of it.

Jack's intuition about places like this led him to tell William, and they came through the door, "William, kindly hand me your wallet…"

The Alibi

"Hello, strangers!" said the bartender in a loud voice for the whole bar to hear. "Are you two fellers lost? You don't seem to be from around here."

Jack could tell the entire room was on edge since the bartender said, "strangers." He tried on a disarming smile and took William's wallet out of the accountant's hand.

"I guess we are lost, in a way, friend," said Jack. He leaned over the counter and slid a silver coin from William's wallet across the bar to the bartender. "We're not here for trouble. We're looking for a guy named Carlos."

"Why?" the bartender asked.

"We think one of his girls is in trouble," Jack answered.

The bartender looked down at the coin before him, then looked up and nodded toward the back table.

Three men sat at the table. Two more prominent men flanked the man in the middle. Jack could barely make out their silhouettes in the dark. He took William by the arm and led him to the three sitting men.

"Good afternoon, fellas," Jack said with a smile. "One of you guys named Carlos?"

William pointed to the man in the middle and said with a tone of recognition, "He is!"

The two men on each end instantly stood up in a defensive stance. They were ready to beat the hell out of anyone who made a sudden move.

Jack threw up his hands and said, "Hey, now! Hey now! Gents, we only want to ask a couple of questions about one of your girls.

"I know a lot of girls. Which one?" said Carlos. He appeared as a middle-aged Hispanic man. He dressed in a natty brown suit, even more tailored than his two strongmen.

"Eloise," said William.

Carlos squinted in the darkness at William. "Eloise? Hey, you were here last night. I told you where Eloise's room was. You looking for a second go-round? You know you have to pay upfront." Carlos then looked at the detective and added, "With two, it's extra…"

"Mr.…Carlos?" Jack began. "This man, Mr. Arbogast, thinks that some harm came to Eloise last night. We came to make sure she's all right."

"She'd better be!" Carlos stated. "She's one of my best earners!"

"Can you show us where her room is?" asked the detective. "Mr. Arbogast has forgotten where it is."

"Okay," Carlos agreed. "If anybody hurt my Eloise, he'll have me and the boys to answer to!"

*

The five men left Blackie's and went down an alley to an old tenement building. They climbed three flights of rickety wooden stairs connected to the side of the brick building to reach the floor where Eloise's room was.

When they reached the door, Carlos immediately began to bang on it, yelling, "Eloise? It's Carlos! Open up! Eloise?"

She did not answer her door. Carlos turned the doorknob and found the door wasn't locked. He rushed in with the rest of the men right behind him. Carlos stopped at the foot of Eloise's bed. He saw the flies had already found Eloise. They were feasting on the blood from the stumps of her arms, legs, and severed head. The sheets from the bed were so saturated with her blood that it was dripping from the bed onto a puddle that ran under it. An upper arm and foot were on the floor as if they had been tossed aside for being in the way of more severing. Eloise's eyes were open. They looked like they were still watching in terror as her body parts were cut away from her one by one and her blood drained to the sheets under her.

"Eloise!" Carlos screamed.

"Oh my God," howled William as he dropped to his knees. "It's true! What I saw in my mind! It's all true!"

An enraged Carlos swung around to William, grabbed him by his coat collar, and pulled him up from the floor. He shook the accountant violently.

"You son of a bitch! You did this to her!" Carlos screamed in William's face. He pulled his right arm back, formed a fist, and punched him across the chin. William was back on the floor immediately. He lay there, crying in shame.

"That's enough, Carlos!" Jack said. "We're here to find out what happened."

Carlos looked around at Jack and said, "You, you little pissant! You probably helped him slice up my Eloise!"

23

Jack realized it was time to make himself known before it was too late. He pulled out his pistol and his badge from his pocket. The gun froze Carlos and his henchmen where they stood.

"I believe an introduction is needed. I'm Detective Jack Banks from the Ninth District. William came into our station and confessed to this murder. But he couldn't have been here. There wasn't enough time to get back to our side of town."

"Well, he was here," said Carlos. "He paid me before I sent him here to get Eloise. And how did he know about killing her if he left her alive?"

"That's a good question, Carlos," Jack answered in a calm voice as not to inflame the situation into something he couldn't control. Pointing the pistol at the three, he continued, "And that's what I'm trying to figure out. Now, if you let me and William go in peace, I'm gonna try to get to the bottom of this."

"I can't let you report this," said Carlos. "A swarm of cops in this building is…bad for business."

Jack considered how to play this. If he were put out of business, Carlos or his ladies wouldn't cooperate much.

"Understood," Jack said. "I can tell my chief we found a bloody bed but no corpse. Then you can handle it the way you need to."

"Get out of my building! And take this scumbag with you!" Carlos said, as he kicked William in the stomach, pulled back his leg again, and kicked him in the face. Carlos then spat at the prone man on the floor.

"C'mon, William," commanded Jack. He looked up at the pimp as he backed out of the room, "Sorry for your loss…"

The detective grabbed the groggy suspect by the back collar. He pulled him through the doorway and shut the door as they hurriedly exited the tenement.

"So much for the South Precinct…" Jack uttered under his breath as he descended the stairs with William.

CHAPTER 3

"I deserved that," William mumbled as he and Jack stood at the station waiting for the subway. He rubbed his right eye socket, which was swelling and growing red. William hung his head in shame and total defeat at his fate.

"You're lucky he didn't break your ribs with that kick," said Jack. He looked at William's red eye and commented, "Yeah, your shiner will probably swell shut before we get back to the station."

"I'm ready to go to jail," William added with an exhausted sigh.

Jack paced in thought behind William. The detective was trying to work out what to say to him next. He rubbed his face and let out an exasperated sigh.

25

"Here's the problem, William. I made a deal with Carlos about not seeing the body to get us out of there," Jack said. "If I keep my word, I'm breaking the law, withholding evidence, and all that crap. But if I pursue the case, there goes the best lead we have as to what really happened. So, I don't know if you're going to jail today."

"I have to, Detective. I don't trust myself alone. What do I have to do to get jailed?" William asked desperately.

"Rob a bank?" Jack answered sarcastically. He placed his hand on William's shoulder and said, "Look, I'll take you home and let you lock yourself in your place. You slide your key under the door to me, and I'll let you out in the morning. Then we'll see what happens tonight. It's kinda like jail…"

"All right," William whispered as he nodded in agreement.

∗

The subway car rolled to a stop in front of them. The two entered and found seats in the middle of the car. They sat together as the subway train began its northbound journey back to the Ninth District.

Jack's mind raced with the evidence that had been presented to him. He had a man confess to a murder that had obviously been committed. He had a witness placing the confessor there. And there was a dismembered body that William had described in his confession. But some things bothered the detective. There wasn't enough time for William to dismember the body and return to his apartment, where he claimed to have woken up. And there wasn't a drop of blood on him.

"Hey, William, judging by seeing the woman's blood splattered everywhere in that room, how did you clean yourself up so fast?"

Jack didn't get an answer from William, so he asked, "William?" to see if he was paying attention.

William's head had slumped forward, resting on his chest. The man was dead asleep. Jack realized William had probably been awake for the last day and night. He decided to let him sleep. Jack reclined in his seat as the train pushed on through the bowels of the city.

*

Suddenly, William was no longer on the subway train. He found himself in the hallway of an apartment building. He wandered down the hall and stood before a door marked 9C. He tried the knob. It turned, but the door was locked with a bolt. With a forceful shove, William pressed his shoulder against the door, broke the door frame, and entered the apartment.

He wandered around the three rooms and found no one there. William made his way to the bedroom and opened the closet door. It was filled with dresses and shoes, verifying that a woman lived there. He stepped into the closet and pulled the door to where it was barely cracked open. And he waited.

A few minutes later, a young woman entered 9C with a bag of groceries. After noticing the broken door frame, she dropped the groceries on the kitchen table and frantically began searching the apartment for intruders. She backed herself to the kitchen sink and retrieved a butcher knife that she had placed in the sink from breakfast.

Her instincts were to yell and get help. But she pressed on through her apartment with the knife in front of her for defense. She slowly inspected the kitchen/sitting room to see if anything had been taken. Nothing was gone or had been touched. As she made her way to her bedroom, she saw the unmade bed and her sleeping gown in a bundle at the foot of the bed. Nothing was out of place. Her pace slowed. Each step was carefully placed as if she were the stalker in this situation.

William watched the woman through the crack of the door. He could feel her fear growing within her. Breathing heavily, she approached the closet to make sure she was alone. That's when William threw the door open and grabbed the knife from her hand. He quickly spun around behind her and took the knife to her throat. Slashing below her jawline silenced the woman's screams as they turned to bloody gurgles. As blood gushed down the woman's chest, it soaked William's arm, too. But he held his grip on the woman till she fainted from the loss of blood. He let go, and she collapsed to the floor. William watched as the woman's life flowed out of her in a series of little spasms, and finally, a rattle came from her mouth and her open throat. He picked up her right hand and, with her bloody butcher knife, began slicing through her wrists…always taking the hands first.

*

The Alibi

The clickety-clack of the subway's wheels against the track, along with the darkened tunnels, had also lulled Jack into a semi-slumber. He yawned, nodded, and tilted his head back to rest it against the window.

Jack was brought out of his semiconsciousness by a hard nudge from William. Still sleeping, William began to moan and convulse. He started waving his hands in front of his body as if trying to fight something off him. William screamed and opened his eyes widely.

Jack grabbed William by the shoulders and tried to control him. "Hey! William! Calm down! What's the matter?"

"She's dead!" William screamed. As he struggled to free himself from Jack, he added, "She's dead, and I killed her!"

"Eloise? William, we know she's dead…" Jack began.

"No! I've killed another woman! Where are we? How far is Morrison Street?" William had broken away from Jack and was now on his feet. Jack thought he might jump off the train.

"Morrison? It's two stops ahead," Jack answered. "Now, c'mon, William, sit down."

"She's there!" William yelled as he resisted the detective's help. "She's on Morrison in Apartment 9C! We have to go there!"

"Alright, alright! Just sit down and don't jump off the train!" Jack ordered William, pulling him down to a sitting position.

"Oh, God! Oh, God! What is happening to me?" William cried.

*

When they emerged from the subway station, William took off at almost a running pace. Jack hurried to catch up with him.

"William, slow down. We'll get there in good time," Jack said as he grabbed William's shoulder to slow his walk.

"It was just like the one before. I could feel everything: the blood, her fear. I could smell the soap she used to wash herself before going to the store. I was there, Detective!" William declared as he pushed Jack aside to continue his quick pace.

William reached the steps of an apartment building. He raced up the stairs and entered the foyer. Jack was right behind him.

"William, how did you know this was the building?" Jack asked.

"I used to live here. Just down the hall from 9C," William answered. He took the stairs and climbed up the nine flights to reach the apartment. All Jack could do was follow him.

They reached apartment 9C. Instinctively, Jack raised his fist to knock on the door. William grabbed the detective's arm and shook his head.

"It's not locked," said William. He pushed against the door, and it opened. Jack could now see the broken door frame where the door had been forced.

"I cut her up, just like Eloise. I cut her up," William mumbled in a mantra-like tone.

"William! Stop!" Jack ordered as he stepped in front of him. "Think a minute, you were on the train with me…asleep! Remember? Maybe you were dreaming?"

"You'll see, Detective," William said weakly.

Jack walked around the small apartment, looking for any sign of struggle or the woman's body. He stopped in front of the small window over the table. He then swiveled around to face William.

The accountant stood in the apartment doorway. He looked down and pointed at the detective's shoes.

Jack looked down to see that he was standing in a pool of blood that had oozed out of the woman's bedroom. Amazed that William was right, he almost didn't want to open the door to the next room. He dreaded what he would find.

The door opened into the bedroom. There, at the threshold, was a severed thigh that had been dismembered at the knee and hip. It was the source of the blood that had run underneath the door. Blood and body parts were strewn across the bedroom. Jack saw parts of feet and arms thrown into the woman's closet. Her head had been propped up between two pillows and was facing the door as if to greet him with a heavy-lidded stare coming from her eyes as he entered. As with the murder of the prostitute, Eloise, the bed appeared to have been used as a cutting table. It was soaking wet with her blood.

"Jesus!" Jack uttered, trying not to get sick at the gory sight. There was no smell of decomposition. The flies had yet to find her. This was a fresh kill.

"William, how did you know about this?" asked Jack, pointing to the bloodied bedroom.

"I didn't know about it, Detective. I did it. With my own hands, I did it, and I couldn't stop…" William said as he collapsed in a living room chair and buried his face in his hands. "I didn't even ask her what her name…"

"Now, goddammit! Cut that shit out right now!" Jack yelled, interrupting William. He had lost his patience with this man. "There's no way you did this! You were on the fucking train with me when this happened."

"And yet, here we are…" William answered, throwing up his hands in defeat.

Jack's yelling had now attracted the attention of an older woman, who appeared at the apartment door. She saw the blood on the floor and began screaming.

"Great!" huffed an exasperated Jack. He ran over to the apartment door and reached into his coat.

"Murderers!" the lady screamed. "Please don't kill me!"

Jack realized the old woman thought he was going for his gun or a knife. He pulled out his badge instead.

"It's alright, lady. I'm Detective Banks of the Ninth Precinct. See? My badge."

The old lady remained apprehensive, unsure whether to trust Jack. She calmed down enough to ask with a tremble in her voice, "What happened to Martha?"

"She met a horrible fate… Missus?" asked Jack.

"Cohen. I'm Mrs. Cohen," she answered. "Oh, Martha…how horrific!"

William's chair had been facing away from the door. He stood up and faced Jack and Mrs. Cohen because he recognized her voice.

"Hello, Mrs. Cohen," said William.

"William Arbogast? Is that you? What are you doing here? What happened to your eye?" asked the perplexed old woman.

William began walking toward the two at the door. With a mournful look on his face, he told her, "I killed her, Mrs. Cohen."

"William! Shut up!' commanded Jack. He turned to the lady and continued. "William is going through a 'hard time,' Mrs. Cohen. We don't know who killed...um, Martha?"

"Yes, Martha Barbier. She had just moved here from France. She was trying to be a dancer," said Mrs. Cohen as she began to weep for her neighbor. "So young...so tragic..."

"Mrs. Cohen," Jack began, "do you have a phone in your place? I need to call this in."

"No," she replied. "But there's a phone in the main lobby downstairs."

"Thank you, Mrs. Cohen," said Jack. He looked back into the apartment and added, "William, come with me."

"What about Martha?" asked Mrs. Cohen.

"This needs to be reported to the local precinct, ma'am. They'll send a squad to take care of her," answered Jack. When William exited the apartment, Jack shut the door. "I'll meet them downstairs and tell them what I know. When they

33

arrive, would you be so good as to let them know who Martha is? That would be very helpful to them and to Martha to find her next-of-kin."

"I'll wait here. I'm not going in there," she said.

"I don't blame you. Thanks for your help, ma'am. C'mon, William."

*

William stood in silence beside Jack and let him call in Martha's murder from the phone in the lobby. When Jack hung up, William followed him through the lobby doors and down the steps to the street to wait for the local police to arrive.

Staying one step behind the detective, William asked, "Now, will you take me to jail?"

Jack froze from walking. He pivoted on one shoe and grabbed William's coat collar. He pulled William to him until their noses were almost touching. The detective's teeth ground together in anger and frustration.

"I can't take you to jail, William," Jack began. "I know you didn't commit this murder. How do I know that? Because I'm your freakin' alibi!"

William broke down and began to cry, "Please, Detective, I don't know what's happening to me. I don't want to kill again! Please help me stop!"

"You're not doing it!" Jack yelled at him. He was so close to William that spittle was showering William's face. "But you seem to know all about it!"

Jack's detective skills flew over the available information he had analyzed. If William wasn't at the scene, someone else was. He nodded at William and asked,

"Accomplice? Is that it, William? Do you know who's committing the murders? Are you in cahoots with the real murderer, and you're just willing to take the rap?"

William shook his head and collapsed to his knees, "No. No. No. No. It's me. I saw it. I did it. Please believe me!"

The crying man folded his body into a ball at Jack's feet. His shoulder heaved with every sob.

Jack looked around at the passing people on the sidewalk. All the detective could think of doing was pulling out his badge and showing it to them.

"Police business!" Jack yelled at the pedestrians who had stopped to look at him and William. "Please, go about yours."

Jack reached down and grabbed the collar of William's coat. He pulled William out of his pathetic ball. The detective decided then and there that William had to be insane. A third party was using William to cover his tracks. William was being manipulated and fed information about these murders. And in his insane mind, he had become convinced that he was committing them. Yes, he was at the scene of Eloise's murder. But what if another person stepped in when William entered her apartment? There had to be another...

"Get up, William. You're making a scene," said Jack as he helped the weeping man to his feet.

Kelly Key

CHAPTER 4

"Nice place, William," said Jack as he walked into the middle of William's living room. His apartment had a living room, a kitchen/dining area, two bedrooms, and a bathroom—a larger, more expensive living space for a person to live alone in the city during the early 1900s. This told the detective that William made a good living as an accountant.

It was neatly kept. Nothing appeared to Jack to be out of place except for the glass of water that sat half empty on the dining table. William had left it there in haste to get to the precinct station early that morning.

"Do you have anything to drink?" asked Jack, sitting in the chair beside the sofa.

"Thank you…and by 'drink' you mean alcohol. I don't drink," William answered softly as he closed his apartment door.

"Of course you don't," commented Jack.

The ride back to Jack and William's part of town had been uneventful. After Jack had reported to the officers who arrived at the grisly murder scene, he escorted William back to the subway and made sure that he stayed awake all the way back.

"That accounting job must pay pretty well," Jack continued. "This is a big place for a single man. You are the only one that lives here, right?"

William was in the middle of hanging up his coat, and he had his back turned to Jack when he answered, "That is correct. I was married, but my wife…died in childbirth…along with the baby, my son."

"Sorry, William," said Jack. "It just said SINGLE on your police report. You should've written WIDOWER."

"It doesn't matter. It's all the same," William said with a bowed head. He shook it to bring himself out of thinking about his dead wife. "I'm sorry, I'm being a bad host. Would you like something to eat?"

"No thanks, William. I'll eat with my…Oh shit! Clemmie!" With everything going on since he had walked into the precinct that morning, Jack hadn't given any thought to food since breakfast with his wife. He looked at his watch, which confirmed that it would be past suppertime by the time he got home.

"Clemmie?" asked William. This was the first time Jack had mentioned her.

"My um, better half," Jack explained as he rose and hurried toward the door. "My better half, who is probably wondering where I am right now. Look, I gotta go. You have enough to eat in here till I come back in the morning?"

"Yes," William confirmed.

"Alright," Jack said as he reached the door and opened it. "Now lock the door and give me the key."

"I'll give you both of them," said William.

"Well then, I'll be back early in the morning. I'll come by before work," the detective said as he walked to the hall and shut the door behind him. He heard the lock click and looked down at the hall's floor. William slid the keys under the door. Jack reached down and scooped them up.

"I got'em, William. You get some rest. I'll see you in the morning."

Jack heard a muffled "Alright" from William on the other side of the door. He turned away from William's apartment door and took one step before stopping. He swiveled back toward the door and tried to open it. It was indeed locked.

"Just checking! See ya, William!" Jack yelled at the door as he placed the two keys in his pants pocket. He then went down the stairs and headed home.

*

Clemmie sat at the kitchen table, rereading Mark Twain's *Adventures of Huckleberry Finn* for the third time. Twain was her favorite author, and she had collected every one of his writings. And "Huck" was her favorite character.

A plate of pasta and meat sauce was kept warm in the oven for Jack. It was so late that Clemmie had already eaten without him. Jack was a detective, and his work often kept him from eating supper with her. Clemmie tried to get used to eating alone, but she missed Jack when he wasn't there. She had already washed the pots and pans and left them to dry beside the sink. So, she waited for Jack by reading about Huck.

Jack opened the door with an expression a dog makes when caught tearing up the sofa. He thought expressing guilt would gain him sympathy.

"I know. Late!" Jack said sheepishly.

"Hey, your plate's in the oven. What do you want to drink?" Clemmie asked with no accusation in her voice.

"I'll get it. Don't get up," Jack answered as he didn't head toward the icebox. Instead, he went directly to the kitchen cabinet and pulled out a bottle of whiskey.

"Bad day?" Clemmie asked, noting his choice of drink.

"Honey, you don't know the half of it," said Jack as he took a swig of liquor directly from the bottle.

Clemmie closed the book and replied, "As a matter of fact, I don't know any of it."

Jack poured himself a glass of whiskey and sat at the table with Clemmie. He hadn't bothered to retrieve his plate of pasta from the oven as he wanted to mellow his mood first.

"I'll spare you the details, Clem. But it was an above-average day. I covered two murders in two different parts of town. Their only connection was this man. This meek, mousy, and quiet little man, who looks like he couldn't harm a fly."

Clemmie couldn't stand it any longer. She got up from the table to take his pasta out of the oven while asking, "You never know about some people. You're a detective. Sometimes, the one least likely to have done it killed the victim, right? So, did he do it?"

Jack's thoughts drifted toward William. He had stared off into space long enough not to notice Clemmie rise and get his dinner. The smell of the pasta brought him back.

"What? Oh, thanks, Clem. I was going to get…" said Jack.

"I asked, did he do it?" said Clemmie as she sat back down.

Jack took another gulp of whiskey. As he swallowed it, he began, "He couldn't have. The timelines for him to be there are all out of kilter. He was always somewhere else. I have a witness who saw him at the location of the first murder, but not at the time it occurred. The second one, he was with me. He has to have a partner. A man can't be in two places at the same time."

"Unless he can split himself in two," Clemmie joked, trying to lighten Jack's mood.

Jack looked up at Clemmie from his glass with sarcastic disapproval.

"Really, Clem?" Jack said with a half-smile on his face.

"There's a smile," Clemmie declared in victory. "I'm just trying to get yourself out of your head."

"It's a lot…" Jack answered.

"You need to worry about him when you clock in in the morning," she said. She leaned over and caressed Jack's face. "Surely there's something else we could talk about."

"Sorry. A detective's work is never done. How was your day?" asked Jack as he dug into the pasta.

"Oh, same old, same old," Clemmie answered with a shrug. "Just another day at the doctor's office. The most exciting thing to happen was that this mom brought her son in. He had fallen down some stairs while playing outside. He broke his arm and cut up his leg…"

Clemmie stopped her recount when she looked at Jack. He was lost in thought again.

As Jack looked at his pasta smothered in tomato sauce, it brought flashes of what he'd witnessed that day. The bloody limbs that were strewn about the room. The blood-soaked mattresses where the murderer had cut the bodies into pieces of flesh. The two pairs of severed hands were both placed by the bed on a table stacked neatly—one over the other—as if they were separate and revered. The victims' cold, dead eyes staring off into oblivion. It made Jack wonder if they saw their own deaths. Jack started to think that maybe eating pasta at this time wasn't the best idea. The visions the pasta gave him weren't conducive to chewing and swallowing it.

"And you're not listening to me again," she admonished him.

Jack's face fell. He pleaded, "Guilty. I'm sorry. Go on, the kid, what happened?"

Clemmie sighed and said, "Never mind. Listen, why don't you finish the pasta and your drink? I'm going to bed."

Jack was confused. He asked, "Bed? It's seven-thirty!"

"Exactly," implied Clemmie with a carnal look in her eye. "For a detective, you're pretty slow at figuring things out."

Clemmie rose from the table and unbuttoned the back of her dress. It became loose, and she let it fall off her shoulders. She turned and headed toward the bedroom door.

At the door, Clemmie stopped. She looked over her shoulder at Jack and said, "Maybe we can find something to talk about in here."

Jack grinned and raised an eyebrow in recognition and anticipation of his wife's suggestion. The liquor in the glass was gone in a gulp. He rose from the table and placed the pasta in the icebox, thinking he might get over his visions and get to it after "talking" to Clemmie. After turning out the lights in the apartment's main room, Jack joined his wife in the bedroom.

He entered the dark bedroom and found that Clemmie had slipped out of her dress. She had carefully laid it on the back of the chair beside the bed and waited for him underneath the bedclothes.

"Now, Detective, let's improve your day," said Clemmie, drawing back the bedsheet to reveal her body to Jack.

"Things are definitely looking up!" Jack responded as he began to unbutton his shirt.

He sat down beside Clemmie and ran his hand down her cheek, then along her neck, and finally to her bare chest. Clemmie sat up and embraced Jack. She kissed him, ran her lips down his neck, and embraced him cheek to cheek.

Clemmie smiled and opened her eyes. Her face was filled with contentment of the moment and her love for Jack. Then, she glimpsed a shape move across the bedroom window. She squinted to make sure what she saw was there. A silhouette of a man kept appearing and ducking away from the window's edge.

Clemmie gasped and pulled herself back. She grabbed the sheet instinctively to cover her naked body.

Confused by Clemmie's withdrawal, Jack asked, "What's wrong?"

A look of fear fell over Clemmie's face. She pointed toward the window and whispered, "There's a man, Jack. A man on the fire escape is looking through the window.

"What?" asked Jack.

Clemmie looked at the window again. The silhouette moved across the window to the other side.

"A man, Jack!" Clemmie whispered loudly. "There he is again!"

Jack spun around. He saw the figure's shadow turn and move towards the fire escape's stairs. Jack leaped to his feet and ran toward the window. He threw the sash up and stuck his head out. He looked down and saw a man on the landing below him.

"Hey! You son of a bitch! Stop! I'm a police officer!" Jack screamed.

The dark figure took off. He descended the stairs two steps at a time.

Jack climbed through the window and gave pursuit. It was a race to the bottom of the fire escape. The black figure had a broad head start. He reached the bottom of the fire escape and climbed down the ladder to the sidewalk. He then took off across the street.

Jack stopped before climbing down the ladder to watch the dark figure. He squinted in the night to see better. He looked at the gait of his running. He'd seen this particular gait before and recognized it. Then he recognized the black coat the figure was wearing— also familiar.

"William?" Jack screamed. "William! Is that you?"

The dark figure stopped running. He turned his head slightly without revealing his face to Jack. Then he took off, disappearing into the night.

"What the hell?" Jack shouted. He reached into his pocket to find the keys to William's apartment and pulled both out to verify that they were in his possession.

The detective turned to climb the stairs to get back to Clemmie as quickly as possible. She had thrown on a gown and looked out the window at Jack as he climbed the fire escape.

"You shouted a name, Jack," said Clemmie. "Did you know who that was?"

Jack was now winded when he reached the fifth-floor landing. Through deep heaves, he said, "I'm not sure. But I think so."

"Who the hell, then?" asked Clemmie.

"The mousy little man I told you about," Jack answered. "I can't believe he followed me home. Listen, I gotta go get him…"

"Oh no, you're not. You're not leaving me here alone. What if he comes back?" Clemmie protested.

Jack was torn about what to do. Clemmie was right about being left alone. The man could circle back, wait for Jack to go, and then come after Clemmie. He could think of only one solution.

"You're right, Clem," Jack began. "Get dressed."

"What? Are you taking me with you?" asked Clemmie.

"No," answered Jack. "I'm taking you to the precinct house where you'll be safe while I go after this loony son of a bitch! Now, come on, Clem! Let's go!"

*

"William! William! I'm coming in!" Jack yelled at William's apartment door as he banged on it. "You better be in there!"

In his rage, Jack fumbled in his pocket to pull out one of William's keys to unlock the door. He left Clemmie in his chief's office and told her he'd return soon. He was sure no one would threaten her with a host of policemen around her.

"Dammit!" Jack cursed at his hand as he pulled one key out and it fell to the hallway floor. He bent over to retrieve it and, before standing back up, shoved the key into the lock and turned it. Jack threw the door open and almost jumped into the apartment.

"William!" Jack yelled as he scanned the apartment. William was sitting in his armchair, with his head thrown back and his eyes shut. He seemed to be muttering something to himself. Jack couldn't make it out. But William was not stirred or awakened by Jack's pounding and yelling. He was oblivious to the world.

Jack stood before William and grabbed him by the shirt with both hands. He shook him violently to wake him.

"William? William!" Jack screamed. "William, wake your ass up!"

The detective was out of patience. He slapped William's face to see if that would rouse him. William moaned and slowly opened his eyes. He rubbed his cheek where he'd been slapped. He appeared confused about when and where he was.

"Detective?" asked a groggy and confused William. "Is it morning already?"

Jack shook the man again to bring him around and asked, "How did you do it? How did you get out of here? Is there another key?"

"What? Get out?" William was utterly baffled by Jack's questions. "I haven't left. I sat down here, and must've fallen asleep, and the next thing I know, you're assaulting me."

Jack let him go and backed off. He scanned the apartment, hoping William had left the key in plain sight. He opened boxes. He opened books. He lifted the cushions on the furniture. No key.

The detective tested the windows—all of them locked. And, unlike in Jack's building, William had no access to a fire escape as the apartment building was old enough not to have one. It was a straight drop down from his window.

"What's all this about, Detective?" asked William.

"I think you know, William," Jack answered. He looked down at his shoes for any sign of water or mud he might have stepped in with his escape. They were spotless and dry. "You're gonna sit there and deny you paid my place a visit tonight."

"What? How? I couldn't leave. I swear on my mother's grave I haven't left this room. I don't even know where you live," William said. He was becoming as frantic as the detective.

Jack took William's black coat from its hook on the wall and dug through the pockets, searching for another key. He found nothing.

"William, I saw this coat on a man running away from my building a couple of hours ago. You're saying it wasn't you? Did you hire somebody to follow me home?"

"What? No! We were together all day. When would I have had time to do that?" William explained. "I swear to you, Detective, I haven't left this room or talked to anyone all night. Please believe me."

"Well, I have a room you can't leave from," Jack said as he threw the coat at William. "Put it on. We're going to the precinct."

"You're arresting me?" William asked while thinking about the irony of getting what he had wished for. "On what charge?"

"Suspected trespassing, voyeurism, and resisting arrest," Jack answered.

"I won't resist. This is what I wanted in the first place," William said as he slipped into his coat.

Jack pushed him through the door and locked it behind him from the hall.

Kelly Key

CHAPTER 5

Chief Dooley had left Clemmie sitting alone in his office while he conducted his duties with the night shift officers around the front desk. She had been in there for over an hour and had no idea when Jack would return to pick her up. She considered the possibility that Jack might not return at all. She loved him. But she did not love the dangers that came along with his job. "Occupational hazard," Jack would joke and laugh it off. It was no comfort to Clemmie.

Although the detective position was sometimes stressful for Jack, it was also stressful for her. She tried not to show her husband that she worried about his safety. But she didn't have to put on that facade when he wasn't around. She watched the clock in the chief's office slowly mark the minutes that Jack was gone.

The chief popped back into his office to retrieve some paperwork. He sat down at his desk to search for the forms.

"Sorry, I'm such bad company. But you know, duty calls. And pulling a double shift doesn't bring out my best social skills," the chief said.

Clemmie managed a small smile as she hugged herself and replied, "It's alright, Chief. I don't need a sitter."

As Chief Dooley continued to pick up sheets of paper from his desk, read them, and toss them back down, he said, "So, you're the reason Jack has started to be late all the time."

Clemmie took a little offense—not at the chief, but at Jack for using her as an excuse.

"Is that what Jack's been telling you?" she asked.

"All the time," Dooley answered. He smiled to defuse the situation and then said, "But now that I've seen you in person, I can understand why."

Clemmie smiled back and blushed a bit. "Thank you," she said.

"Now, don't get me wrong. Just because I understand it doesn't mean I'm going to let it pass," he chided.

"I'll try to get him up earlier," Clemmie said. She tried to joke back at the chief.

Dooley continued to read papers. He switched his search to the top drawer of his desk. "Now, where did he run off to have to leave you here? He was in such a hurry that I didn't get to ask."

"He said he recognized the Peeping Tom watching us from our fire escape. He said he knew where he lived," Clemmie said with dread, remembering the sight of the dark figure outside her bedroom window.

"Damn fool," Dooley declared. "He should have taken an officer with him for backup."

"Jack didn't think the guy would give him any trouble," she explained. "He said the guy was kind of 'mousey.'"

The chief scanned the paper in his hand and nodded. "Found it!" he exclaimed. He rose from his desk and headed toward his office door. He patted Clemmie on the shoulder as he passed and added, "Well, if he brings him in, we'll take care of him. I gotta go book some rat bastard."

"Okay," Clemmie said as he left her to stare at the clock again and worry some more.

Then she could hear Jack's big voice approaching the precinct from outside. She heard him say, "No, William," and "Shut up, William."

When Jack entered the main room with William Arbogast, Clemmie rose from the chief's chair and stood in the doorway to watch Jack. Her husband didn't look her way as he escorted Arbogast to the big front desk. He appeared as if he were a man on a mission.

Sitting behind the desk, Officer Morrison looked disgusted, like a policeman who was just about to finish his shift when more work was piled in front of him. He looked down at William to size him up.

"You're working late, Detective," Morrison stated sarcastically, implying that Jack shouldn't be there at all, especially when he brings in more work for the officer.

"Well, you know, a detective's work is never done. I'm officially not on the clock. But this one made me come back," replied Jack.

"This feller doesn't look like he could harm a fly. What's the charge?" asked the officer.

"Charge-es," Jack corrected Morrison. "I'm starting with suspected trespassing, voyeurism, and resisting arrest. Maybe I can think of some more when I get back in the morning. William's been a bad boy tonight."

"I didn't do anything. I was home all night," William said, defending himself.

"That's what they all say," Morrison said, wearily sighing. "Foley! Take Mr. Arbogast and start processing him. I'll start the paperwork…"

Jack handed William over to the officer and told the accountant, "You're getting what you want, William. And you better stay there."

"Detective!" Chief Dooley said in a raised voice. "A moment?" he continued as he walked toward his office door.

Jack followed his boss into the office and finally saw Clemmie. They tightly embraced as Chief Dooley shut the office door.

"Is that him?" asked Clemmie. "Did you get him?"

"That's William," Jack replied. "He says he didn't leave his apartment. But he's wearing the same coat as our peeper. It's got to be him."

"Sit down, Banks," Dooley commanded. He took his chair and sat down behind his desk.

Jack quickly hugged Clemmie, and both sat down in the two chairs facing the Chief. Clemmie scooted the chair closer to Jack and took his hand.

"Isn't this man the same guy from this morning?" Dooley asked. "I thought I told you to dump him on the South Precinct."

"Well, Chief, things got complicated. It's been a long day…" Jack said.

"Long day? If you'll notice, I'm still here when I should be shooting the shit down at Clancy's!" Dooley said. "Where were you all day?"

"Chief, this is the strangest guy I've ever been around," Jack began. "He claims he can see murders as they happen. He's confessed to doing the deeds. But he's not there when the murders are committed. I know, because he was sitting beside me when one of the women was killed."

"Just how were they killed?" asked the chief.

"Well…" Jack looked at Clemmie. He had tried to spare her the gory details of what he had seen that day.

Clemmie understood what the look he gave her was about. She shook her head condescendingly at her husband and said, "Jack, I'm a nurse. I think I can take a bloody story."

"The perpetrator cut them up," Jack began slowly, trying to decide how much to reveal. "The limbs were severed at the joints—knees, hips, elbows, and shoulders. Both heads were sliced off, with their eyes kept open. And the hands…they were placed, almost reverentially, together on the table."

"Why?" asked the chief.

"I dunno, Chief. Maybe the guy's got a hand-kink. Nobody was there to give a motive. Nor was there a note," Jack answered. "Anyway, that's the gist of what I saw today. Two women butchered alive…"

"Oh my God," Clemmie whispered. Now she knew why Jack had gone straight for the whiskey when he got home.

"And your man claims to have witnessed both killings?" asked the chief.

"He claims to have done them. Chief, I know he couldn't have. Especially the second one from today. I was with him the whole time. I've got witnesses saying that he was at the first one, but not at the time of the murder. He's got to have help—a partner. Nobody can be in two places at once."

"Well, he seems to be involved," began the chief. "Seems he knows too much not to be."

"And there was tonight…" Clemmie added.

"Oh, we were in our bedroom when Clemmie saw somebody out the window on the fire escape. I chased him down the stairs." Jack said.

"Did you see his face?" asked the chief.

"No. But he ran just like Arbogast. Then I recognized the coat. The exact one he was wearing tonight when I brought him in. I shouted his name, and he stopped running. He was about to turn to face me, then ran off," said Jack. "That's when I brought Clemmie here and went to get Arbogast. He claims he was asleep and never left his apartment. He denies he was at my window."

The chief got up from his chair to pace behind his desk. "Do you think he would tell you if he had done it or known about it?"

Jack nodded, "He's told me everything else—where the bodies were, how they were chopped up. He wants to confess. So, I don't know why he would deny the last part."

Dooley turned around from his pacing and stopped. "Sounds like a twin situation to me. One tells the other what's going to happen, then the other twin shows up."

"So why is he confessing to crimes he's not committing?"

"Crazy?" guessed the chief. "Protecting his brother? Seems to be a stupid way to have an alibi. Maybe this twin has something on this Arbogast? Making him confess so the other one gets off?"

"That's one of the reasons I brought him in, Chief," said Jack. "We'll know for sure it's not him if another lady gets chopped up."

"Well, he's not going anywhere tonight," said the chief.

*

After being fingerprinted, William was still wiping the ink off his fingers as Officer Foley took him by the arm down a hallway that led to the holding cells. Foley picked an empty one, unlocked the barred door, and guided William inside. William turned to face the officer as he locked the door.

"I'd get to sleep if I were you," advised Foley. "They serve breakfast pretty early here."

"Thank you, Officer," William answered. His voice expressed genuine gratitude toward the policeman. He was finally in a space that felt safe to him. A place where he will be watched constantly. For the first time in weeks, William felt himself relax.

He turned and walked toward the bed on the opposite wall. William removed his coat and neatly folded it in half. He placed it at the foot of the bed. Then, he sat on the bed, neglecting to pull down the brown blanket. He reclined, and as his head hit the pillow, William placed his right arm underneath it to give more support to his head. After looking at the ceiling momentarily, he closed his eyes and instantly fell asleep.

*

Jack helped Clemmie put on her coat. She was ready to leave and go home. She'd heard enough of violence to do her a while.

"Let's get out of here, Jack," Clemmie said. "No offense, Chief, but this place gives me the creeps."

"None taken," the chief answered. "This place is for the lowlifes of society. And the criminals are worse!"

"Thanks, Chief!" Jack responded, feigning to be hurt by the words.

Dooley smiled and told Clemmie, "Take that one home, miss. And make sure he's on time in the morning!"

"No promises!" Jack said as he led Clemmie toward the office door.

Clemmie turned and smiled as she went through the door, "Thank you, goodnight."

Jack escorted Clemmie towards the precinct's front entrance. He turned and waved at the officer at the desk.

"Night, Morrison!" Jack said.

"And don't come back!" the officer answered, never looking up from the paperwork in front of him.

"Nice!" responded Jack.

Just as the couple was about to walk out, Officer Foley stuck his head out of the door that went back to the holding cells.

"Hey, Detective!" shouted Foley to stop Jack and Clemmie from leaving. "You'll want to look at this before you go!"

Both Clemmie and Jack sighed. They looked at each other knowingly.

"Let's go, Jack. I want to go home," Clemmie pleaded.

Jack hesitated at the door. He relented to the officer's request.

"It'll be a second, Clem. I promise. I'll be right back!" Jack kissed her on the cheek and left her waiting for him at the door.

*

Foley led Jack to Cell 9, which was where William was being held. They stopped in front of the door and looked at William writhing on the bed. He appeared to be asleep, but was struggling at the same time. He said nothing, save for a few grunts and gurgling sounds.

"Have you ever seen anything like that?" asked Foley. "He's either on drugs or having some sort of fit!"

"I've heard him talk in his sleep. But nothing like this," Jack answered. "William, WILLIAM! Wake up!"

Upon hearing Jack's voice, William stopped convulsing. It was like a switch had been thrown inside his body. William opened his eyes and turned his head toward the policeman and Jack.

"Detective? I thought you'd left," said William as he sat up on the bed. "What's wrong? Are you releasing me?"

"You're not being released. I should be the one asking what's wrong, William. Were you having a nightmare?"

William looked down and thought for a minute, "I have no memory of one. What happened?"

"You were throwing some sort of fit. You don't remember what could have made you do that?" asked Jack.

60

"No," William answered. "I'm sorry I caused concern..."

Jack sighed and told William, "Get some rest." He then turned to Foley, "I'm going home."

"Oh, before you go, Detective," William began as he looked up from the floor. At that moment, what appeared to be a shadow fell over his face. For the first time, William smiled. It wasn't from happiness. It looked sinister. Something had changed. He continued,

"You have a beautiful wife. What a lucky man you are..." said William with the smile still on his face.

A chill ran over the detective. Jack didn't know how to answer this change in William. He took a step back from the cell door and told Foley, "Keep an eye on him, will ya? I'll be back in the morning."

Jack left the cell area in a hurry. He wanted to get to Clemmie and get her home as quickly as he could. Reaching the front, he grabbed Clemmie's arm.

"Let's get out of here,' Jack told his wife.

Clemmie could see something had happened to Jack in the cell area. She asked, "Jack? What's wrong?"

Jack was now giving his better half almost a bum's rush to get her out of the precinct. He answered, "Tell ya later. Let's go!"

*

They had walked back to their apartment building in hurried silence. Jack wanted Clemmie inside as quickly as possible. William's statement about Clemmie had left Jack paranoid. If there was a second man, he might've been following them home. The detective was making himself keenly aware of his surroundings.

"Jack, wait a minute," Clemmie finally ordered as the quick pace was tiring her. She stopped walking so he would stop, too.

"Are you going to tell me why we're practically running home?" she asked. "What got you so spooked back there?"

Jack thought for a minute. He was going to tell her enough to satisfy her curiosity.

"William was having some sort of convulsive fit. When he came out of it...he was a different man. The look on his face had changed. It was...menacing in tone. I've never seen him like that."

"Did he threaten you?" asked Clemmie. She placed her hand on his shoulder to calm him.

Jack paused before he told her. "Kinda. I thought getting home and safe was a good idea. He'd worn me out today. I was ready to get away from him."

"That's what I've been telling you, Jack," she said. "Clock out every once in a while."

Jack smiled at his wife and agreed, "You're right. Let's get home."

The first thing Clemmie did when she reached the bedroom was close the curtains. There'd be no more peeping tonight.

The first thing Jack did was pour himself a double shot of whiskey. After downing it with one gulp, he joined his wife in the bedroom. The last thing he did, after turning off the lights, was place his service revolver under his pillow.

CHAPTER 6

Camila and Mateo were used to sitting in the dark. Their mother, Carlotta, could barely afford the one-room apartment they lived in. Her man—the children's father—had left her after both were born. He was a charmer, not a father.

After her twelve-hour shift in the garment district, Carlotta supplemented her small income by entertaining men at night in her room. To give herself privacy with the "john" (and hide her shameful sinning from her children), Carlotta would lead Camila and Mateo to the room's closet.

They were instructed not to make a sound while their mother "chatted" with her male friends. This led to many late-night hours spent by the brother and sister sitting in the dark, listening to the shuffles and groans just outside the closet door. Sometimes the two would fall asleep and have to be carried to bed after their mother's last appointment for the night.

"You weren't supposed to work tonight," whined Camila. "I hate the closet."

"I do, too!" added the younger Mateo.

"I know. I know, mi chocitos," answered Carlotta as she cleared the supper table. "But I just have the one friend tonight. You might not be in there that long. This one's an older man. Maybe I can hurry him along," Carlotta added, not going into any specific meanings for her children.

"There's nothing to do in there," Camila protested.

"Yes, and her feet stink," Mateo said, pointing to his sister. He quickly received a slap on the hand from Camila for saying it.

"When are you going to stop seeing your friends, Mama?" asked Camila.

"Soon. I want to stop seeing them as much as you two do. Now, no more whining. Let's go."

There was a faint knock on the door. Carlotta's "friend" stood on the other side of it. After a minute, he rapped again.

"He's here!" the mother declared in a whisper. "He's early! Go on to the closet! I'll try to get rid of him as quick as I can!"

"Yes, Mama," the brother and sister said. Resigned to their place, they slid out of the chairs at the table and went into the closet.

Carlotta shut the closet door and heard the soft wrapping at her door again. She forced a smile on her face and yelled, "Coming!"

*

Camila and Mateo sat facing each other in the pitch-blackness inside the closet. Their only light source came from the slit of a crack between the bottom of the closet door and the floor. They would always choose not to listen to the muffled conversation between their mother and her man-friends.

This night was different. After a few minutes of conversation, the siblings began hearing sounds of shuffling feet and furniture. These sounds differed from the standard tussling and babbling from their mother's bed. Stifled grunts and groans seeped in from underneath the door. They could hear their mother trying to scream through a covered mouth. They grabbed each other's hands and pulled themselves closer, and the struggle went on just outside the closet door.

They finally heard Carlotta utter words they could understand. It increased their fear.

"Please! I have children!" Carlotta pleaded.

After one final gurgled scream from beyond the door, Camila and Mateo heard silence fall from the room. They obeyed their mother's order and remained motionless. After the older sister held a finger to her lips to get her brother to be silent, they hugged each other, daring not to make a sound, save for their labored breathing. Absolute fear and dread pumped through their little hearts, not knowing what to do next.

Then, there was a sound. The sound of heavy leather shoes walking on the wooden floor of the apartment. They heard it grow louder and louder as the footsteps approached the closet. The walking stopped. Camila and Mateo looked down at the crack at the bottom of the door. The shadow of two feet was there. They started to shiver, struggling not to make a sound.

The door slowly creaked open. The siblings looked upon the dark silhouette of a man standing in the doorway. A bloody butcher knife hung from his right hand. In an instant, the dark man was upon the children.

*

After a fitful night of sleep, Jack woke up at five the next morning. He lay in bed on his back, staring at the ceiling. He thought about the previous day's events and attempted to make sense of them. This was a challenging task. Jack had never had a case like this one. He had a man in custody who he knew hadn't committed murder. Nevertheless, women were dead. Somebody was out there hacking women up and leaving their bloody bodies carved up in pieces.

Whether William Arbogast had committed the crimes or had known someone who did was yet to be determined. What made Jack lose sleep that night was William's last comment about Clemmie. It wasn't a direct threat but an insinuation. William knew what Clemmie looked like and where she lived. For the first time since he had made detective, he felt he had put his wife in danger.

He felt determined to figure out what was going on as quickly as possible…for Clemmie's sake.

Jack stretched his arms and sat up in bed. Then he remembered the revolver under his pillow. He pulled it out and placed it on the bedside table.

"You're up?" asked Clemmie groggily. "It's early."

Clemmie rolled over to Jack's side of the bed to cuddle against his back. She yawned and stroked his back, and then continued through a yawn, "You want breakfast? Or something else…?"

Jack smiled at the offer. He stood up from bed and answered, "Thanks, Clem. But I'd better go on in. I want to check on William."

"You married to him or me?" asked Clemmie playfully, still hoping for some "Jack time."

Jack smiled again, "I know where my bread's buttered. But last night raised some flags we can't ignore. If William does have an accomplice, it's a good bet that he knows about me…and you, now."

"William's locked up. How could he tell anybody about us?"

"None of this makes sense, honey," he answered. "I've never let any perpetrator get this close before. Hey, maybe it's a good idea for you to visit your mother for a few days…till I can figure this out?"

Clemmie sat up in bed and asked, "You think it's that serious?"

"Clemmie, if you had seen what I saw yesterday, you wouldn't think twice about a threat. There's someone out there who's pure evil. I want to catch him to get him off our backs."

Jack leaned down to his wife, kissed her on the forehead, and said, "Your mother's place isn't too far. In fact, it's closer to the precinct house. I'm not telling you what to do. But I am asking you, for my peace of mind?"

Clemmie sat up on Jack's side of the bed. She thought about last night. She thought about looking up and seeing the dark figure in the window watching her. She was beginning to believe that her husband was right. His suggestion would solve a problem.

"Just for a few days?" she asked.

"It may not take that long," Jack said, putting on his pants. "William's either going to crack and confess or name his accomplice. The man's on the edge of insanity. I just hope we get answers before he loses touch with all reality."

Clemmie nodded, "Just for a few days, then."

"Promise!" said Jack. He hugged Clemmie and kissed her. "Call the station and let me know when you get there?"

"Alright," she said. She hugged him and didn't want to let him go.

He rubbed her cheek, and a thought popped into his head. "I still have the pasta from last night in the icebox! You don't have to make breakfast."

"You sure can kill a moment, Jack," Clemmie said as she smacked his chest playfully.

Jack smiled at his wife and put on his shirt. He kissed her forehead before heading to the icebox.

*

Even at the early hour when Jack arrived at work, the precinct house was abuzz with activity. Jack sensed something was going on. He went up to the main desk, where Sergeant Foster was talking to one of the jailers.

"What's all the hubbub, Sergeant?" Jack asked.

"Just the man we're looking for. Your nutcase back there has gone mental. He keeps asking for you."

"Me? Why?" Jack asked.

The sergeant leaned back in his chair and told him, "Aw, he threw some fit early this morning. Started wailing and screaming. He was banging his head against the door, calling out your name. We had to go in and restrain him to keep him from killing himself."

Jack shook his head and commented, "Welp, start the day right! Guess I'd better get back there and talk to him."

The jailer unlocked the door that led to the cells, and Jack followed him to the one holding William. The detective found William in a straitjacket, lying on his side in a fetal position on the bed. As he was facing the wall, he didn't acknowledge Jack's presence. But he kept calling for him.

"Detective Banks…Detective Banks…" William muttered repeatedly.

The jailer unlocked the cell door, and Jack nodded in gratitude. As the jailer locked the door behind him, Jack stepped over to the bed and stood over the balled-up William.

"William? William! It's me. I'm here," said Jack. He grabbed William by the shoulder and waist and rolled him over on his back. Jack saw the huge knot on Arbogast's forehead with a gash in the eyebrow beneath it. This was on top of the beating wounds given by Carlos. The eye below that was beginning to swell shut.

"Ah, William, what did you do?" Jack asked, examining the eye.

William slowly opened his eyes. He realized Jack was standing over him.

"Detective?" he asked softly. William immediately began to weep. "Detective, kill me! Please! Kill me!"

"What's got into you, William?" Jack asked as he grabbed the front of the straitjacket to pull the sobbing soul to a sitting position on the bed. Then he sat down beside him.

"Nobody's going to kill you, William," said Jack. "Now, can you calm down and tell me what's going on?"

William shook his head in an attempt to stop crying. "I'm evil, detective. I can't stop. Even this cell can't stop me," William swallowed hard and looked the detective in the eye. He continued haltingly, "This time...I killed the children...I couldn't stop. They were there...with her. I had to kill them! I'm a monster!"

William broke down into another blubbering mess. Jack rose to pace in front of the wailing man on the bed. The more William cried, the angrier and more frustrated Jack became. His pacing quickened with his rising rage. He stopped in front of William and smacked his cheek.

The shock of the slap jolted William back from the black hole of sorrow he had been wallowing in. Jack grabbed the sobbing man by the face with both hands, so William had no choice but to look at him.

"Listen, William," Jack said through gritted teeth. "You didn't kill any kids. You didn't kill another woman. Where are you, William? You're in a goddamn jail cell in the ninth precinct! You didn't leave this cell all night. Now, think, Mr. Arbogast. Use that analytical accountant brain inside your noggin. You. Didn't. DO IT!"

It was like talking to a brick wall. William stared blankly into Jack's eyes as if Jack hadn't said a word to him. "She begged for her life. She told me she had children. Why did she tell me, Detective? If she hadn't told me, I wouldn't have known about the children!"

William started sobbing again. Jack let go of William's face and backed away before he hit him again. He was seething in frustration.

"I'll tell ya, William, I think you're insane. I also think you have an accomplice out there who's actually doing the killing. Here's the deal. You tell me who it is, then I'll stop him from killing any more kids."

The crying man before Jack stopped. He lifted his chin off his chest and nodded his head.

Jack braced for William to break and tell all. He knelt in front of him so that he was at the same level as William's eyes and waited for him to speak.

William cleared his throat, "It's me. I did it. I saw it. I was there. I killed the children. Kill me!"

"Go to hell, William!" Jack yelled. He'd lost his patience with the accountant. "Nate!" he yelled, calling the jailer to come unlock the door. He turned from the door and said to William, "I'm leaving now. And as far as I'm concerned, you can stay in that wraparound coat till you're ready to tell me your racket. Have a good day, Mr. Arbogast."

Just as the jailer began to unlock the door, William muttered, "43 Chestnut Street."

Jack turned and asked, "What did you say?"

"I was at 43 Chestnut Street. Apartment G. You'll find the children in the closet..." William began to cry again at the thought of the slain little ones.

*

Jack left William with his tears. He exited the jail cells and went straight to the precinct map to find Chestnut Street. It was at the north end of the precinct, but still within walking distance. He found the police roster and saw that it was Eddie Finnegan's beat. As it was still early in the morning, he had to wait for the officers' morning meeting with the chief to end before talking to him.

The policemen filed out of the meeting room, and Jack spotted Eddie. He waved at him to talk to him.

"Officer Finnegan! A word?" Jack requested.

The officer heard him and made his way through the gaggle of cops who were separating to start their shifts. "Morning, Detective," the young officer began. "You're here early," he said with a wry grin.

"My reputation precedes me," Jack answered, getting the officer's sarcastic remark about his chronic tardiness. "How was the morning meeting?"

Eddie snickered. "Listening to the chief ramble on for 45 minutes about outsmarting the thugs out there? A wonderment."

"Dooley's been known to…elaborate," Jack commented.

"I'd call it droning," Eddie said.

"Don't I know it. Let's take a walk," Jack said, taking the officer by the arm and leading him toward the door.

"So, all this small talk was to get me to come with you?" Eddie asked as he tried to keep up with the detective, who walked at a good pace away from the precinct house.

"I'm a charmer," Jack joked. "You're ready to start your patrols. C'mon, I want to check something out on your beat. What can you tell me about Chestnut Street?"

"Chestnut? It's pretty skeevy," commented the officer. "Why do you want to go to the poor Latin area of town?"

Jack opened the precinct's door to the outside and said, "Um, my new best friend in the holding area gave me an address. I want to see if he's telling the truth."

Officer Eddie stopped on the sidewalk. "The crazy guy? What's up with him anyway? I heard he kept the jailers awake all night last night."

"How rude of him," Jack answered. It was his way of joking that it was the jailers' job to be awake on their shift. "Call him crazy but he's not been wrong about anything since I met him. Well, except for claiming that he killed the victims. He couldn't have killed the last one. Let's go and get this over with."

*

The Latin District was as vibrant and colorful as it was poor. Many immigrants came from the Caribbean islands, bringing their cultures with them. The streets were teeming with Spanish-speaking people. It was an environment Jack was unfamiliar with—and one of the main reasons he wanted Officer Finnegan to accompany him. It was odd that the chief assigned someone of Irish descent to a beat where most residents spoke Spanish.

"How did you get this assignment anyway?" Jack asked, checking the street signs to find Chestnut Street.

"What? Oh. My dad's Irish but my mother is Puerto Rican. I got Dad's looks and both of them's Catholicism," Finnegan answered.

"That makes sense," said Jack. "Here's Chestnut. It's where William said the murder happened."

74

"Watch your back," Finnegan commented. "This is a tough street—even in the daylight."

Jack and Officer Finnegan found 43 Chestnut. It appeared to them that the building had once been an old hotel, now converted into a tenement building. Out of every open window hung various pieces of clothing, including underwear, drying in the sun. To people this poor, modesty could not be afforded.

The two men went through the lobby and up the old stairs, eventually standing before the door of Apartment G. Finnegan reached for the doorknob, and Jack reached out to stop him.

"Fair warning, Eddie. If William's right about this, what we're about to walk into will be grisly, to say the least," said Jack.

Eddie smiled reassuringly and said, "Detective, this is the Latin part of town. These people live desperate, poor lives. People get killed here over bread. I've seen plenty of dead bodies…"

Jack shrugged and let go of the officer's arm. Finnegan tried the doorknob. It wasn't locked. The door opened inward.

"Sweet Mary and Jesus!" Finnegan exclaimed as he looked upon the carnage that once was Carlotta. Like the other victims, she had been dismembered at the joints, and her head had been placed on the table facing the door. Beside her head were her hands, placed delicately on top of each other.

The officer stood in the doorway in utter horror at the blood and gore scattered around the small one-room tenement. He stood there, not moving.

Jack had grown impatient. He knew if the woman was there, then the kids were probably there, too. Then Jack saw that more blood was oozing from under the closet door.

"Dammit all to hell! One side, Eddie! I gotta get to the closet!" Jack told the officer as he shoved his way into the room.

The detective walked hurriedly but carefully across the floor, still wet with Carlotta's blood. He reached the closet door and threw it open. There, on the closet floor, lay Camila and Mateo.

"Aw, dammit, William. I wish you had been wrong. Eddie! Get in here!" Jack said as he squatted down to look at the bodies of the children.

The killer had not dismembered them. They were stabbed and left to bleed out as the killer still had to carve up their mother. Mateo was on top of his sister. His eyelids drooped as if he were half asleep.

Eddie steeled himself to make it past Carlotta's head and across the room. He joined Jack at the closet door.

"Look at the boy's forearms. They're all slashed. Looks like he put up a fight defending his sister. Poor kid," Jack said. He then lifted the dead Mateo off his sister.

When the boy was lifted, Jack heard a soft moan. Camila was still breathing.

"Holy shit! Eddie! Go get help!" Jack yelled as he looked around the closet to find something to stop Camila from bleeding to death.

76

CHAPTER 7

Jack and Officer Finnegan had taken Camila to a nearby hospital. She had survived but was still in a state of shock from the trauma and blood loss. The small girl slipped in and out of consciousness.

Her deep wounds were many, but not fatal. The child would have died if Jack had not found her. Or, if William hadn't told Jack where to find her.

Jack had remained at the hospital, hoping Camila would live. He had told Finnegan to return to the station and let them know his location in case Clemmie tried to contact him. He sat out in the hall next to the girl's room doorway while the doctor worked on her. First, the nurse emerged from the room. She walked away so fast that Jack hardly had time to notice her, get up, and ask her a question.

"Hey! Nurse! What's going on?" Jack yelled down the hall after the fast-walking nurse. She didn't break her stride to answer him. "I'm an officer of the law, you know. I can have you arrested for…ignoring a policeman!"

"Detective, please keep your voice down," Dr. Benson chided Jack as he gently pulled Camila's door closed.

"Finally! Somebody who talks to me!" Jack said, lowering his voice. He had finally realized how loud he was. He next whispered, "What about it, Doc? Is she gonna live?"

Dr. Benson sighed and said, "Well, I've done all I can. She's lost a lot of blood. I sewed up the wounds. It's up to her now. What kind of person would do something like this? A whole family…"

"You don't know the half of it, Doc," answered Jack. "This guy's evil, sadistic, and meticulous. He chops up people and makes them watch while he cuts on them."

"Then it doesn't make sense. If he's that horrific, what made him stop with the children?" the doctor asked.

"It's my theory he wanted a witness. Somebody to survive to tell about him," answered Jack.

"Out of the mouths of babes…" the doctor quoted. "Sick."

"That's what I think she's alive to do. Can I talk to her?" Jack asked.

"You mean 'interrogate her'?" the doctor answered with raised eyebrows. "I can't allow it now. Besides, we've got her sedated. Even if she did rouse up, she'd be so drugged that you could take everything she said with a grain of salt. Perhaps…tomorrow…"

"C'mon, Doc. She's the only witness…" Jack pleaded.

"Tomorrow!" Dr. Benson said sternly. "My advice to you is to go back to work or go home. Staying here won't make a difference tonight. She'll either make it…or not. It depends on how strong her little body is."

Jack sighed, "Alright, if you say so, Doc. Please have somebody call the station if she revives, huh?"

The doctor shook his head, "We'll see."

*

Jack left the hospital more frustrated than ever. None of what was happening made any sense to him. As he walked down the street, he decided to go back to William's apartment to look for anything that would help to make sense of it all. He still had the keys William had given him. And as far as the legality of entering the place, Jack's thinking was that, with William's mental state, he probably would never see that apartment again. He'll either be incarcerated or dead by his own hand.

The detective unlocked William's apartment door and immediately searched for any documents William might have written. Jack was looking for any journal, diary, or personal correspondence that might give insight into Arbogast's mental state. The only thing remotely related to any papers with personal handwriting was stacks and stacks of accounting ledgers next to William's desk in the corner.

Jack scoured through the ledgers and was, at first, impressed with William's precise and detailed record keeping. But as he continued to look through the legers, the newer ones grew sloppier and more erratic. He picked up the last ledger, dated from the previous month, and opened it. There were no names or numbers written in the lines of the pages. William had made sharp lines of jagged angles up and down the pages. There were no words, only the lines. It looked like the accountant had held the pencil as if it were a knife. The pages had holes and ruts in them, revealing how hard he had pressed the pencil to the paper.

"William, William, William…" Jack sighed as he closed the last ledger and tossed it on top of the stack. "Even the bats in your belfry are crazy."

Jack sat down at the accountant's desk. The desktop was clean of any papers. As erratic as William's mind had become, he was still tidy. He tried the drawers. The ones on the side opened, revealing files and documents—records that are the tools of the accounting trade. The detective found nothing out of the ordinary in them, just proof that he was a busy accountant.

The middle drawer was not as giving. It was locked. Jack ran his hand under the drawer in search of a hidden key…no luck. Rising to the rank of detective meant that he had dealt with many robbers over the years. He had picked up a few tricks of the trade. He reached for the letter opener with a long blade that was on the desk in a holder. In two seconds, the detective had jiggered the lock and pulled the drawer open.

Lying on top of assorted papers, checkbooks, and matches was something that caught Jack's eye. It was a photograph of William and a woman that Jack could only assume was William's wife. The picture showed them sitting on a sofa, holding hands and looking into each other's eyes. William was doing something in the shot that Jack had never seen him do. He was smiling. Seeing William happy made Jack smile, too.

Jack was ready to put the photo back. However, as he proceeded to place it back on the pile of papers and checkbooks, he thought of two words: Camila and Witness. Jack drew back his hand and slipped the photo of William and his wife into his coat pocket.

Jack returned to his empty apartment. He wanted to see Clemmie in the worst way possible. But he dared not visit her for fear of leading the killer to her mother's place. It was best to let the stalker/man out there think that they were both still at home. And if he decided to pay another visit, Jack would be ready for him. He retrieved the bottle of whiskey from the cabinet and set it on the table. He laid his revolver right beside it. Jack slept at the kitchen table that night.

*

As Clemmie walked the last few blocks to work that next morning, she worried about her husband. Not so much for his safety; she knew he could defend himself. She was concerned about his mental state and the toll this "William" character was taking on him. Jack was spending too much time on this one man...or two men. She thought he was becoming exhausted and strung out. Then, right on cue, she rounded the corner, and there sat Jack on the steps of the doctor's office where she worked.

Clemmie didn't hesitate to run to her husband. Jack saw her and stood just as Clemmie reached him. They gave each other a clinched hug that lasted a long while. Clemmie then kissed her husband and asked Jack, "So, how's things?"

Jack chuckled, not letting go of her, and said, "Oh, about as well as can be expected."

"That bad, huh?" Clemmie joked back. "No, seriously, are you okay? You look awful. Didn't you sleep any?"

"Sort of," Jack said. "I kept vigil in the apartment last night. The kitchen table makes a lousy pillow…"

"Jack," Clemmie chided. "Promise me you'll take care of yourself. Sleep at the Precinct house if you have to. When that guy sees that we're not there, he'll stop coming."

"You're right, Clem," he agreed. Then he tried to change the subject. "How's Edna?"

"Mother's as ornery as ever. A joy to be around," Clemmie said. "How much longer do you think we'll have to do this?"

"William tried to kill himself yesterday. He's either fully insane now or close to it. He'll either die or go to the madhouse. So I don't know how much longer he'll be around," answered Jack.

"Well, I say the quicker the better. Good riddance," Clemmie said. "That man's brought nothing but pain and suffering to everyone—especially you."

"Listen," the detective began. "I have to get to the hospital. There's a chance a victim might be able to see me this morning."

"Another one of his victims?" she asked.

"He was in a straitjacket when this attack happened. So, no. But he knew about it," Jack answered. "I wish I could figure out how he knows about the killings."

"Find that out, and I can come home," Clemmie answered, hugging him.

"I'm trying my best…" said Jack. He gave Clemmie a long kiss and, when they separated, said, "I gotta go. I love you so much."

"Show it by coming back to me. And get some rest, will ya? I love you, too!" she said as she slapped Jack's chest—a love tap.

Jack walked Clemmie up the steps and to the door of the doctor's office. They embraced, and Clemmie gave Jack a peck on the cheek. Jack cupped her face in his hand and let it slip off as he descended the steps. Before he got to the corner, he looked back, and there was Clemmie at the door watching him. He smiled at her and turned the corner.

*

"I'm looking for Dr. Benson?" Jack asked the clerk at the hospital's front entrance.

"His office hours are ten till twelve and one till four," the clerk answered.

Jack was in too much of a hurry to deal with hospital bureaucracy. He reached into his coat pocket and produced his badge. "I'm not a patient of his. I'm Detective Banks from the Ninth Precinct. Apparently, I need to get his permission before I can interview one of his patients?"

The clerk rose from his seat to get a closer look at Jack's badge. He looked up from the badge at Jack and said, "Well, Detective, I'm sure he's here somewhere. He's usually doing rounds at this hour."

"Thanks," said Jack as he stuffed his badge back in his coat pocket. He blew past the clerk to head to Camila's room. When he got to the room's door, he saw Dr. Benson was already in there, standing over Camila's bed. Jack politely knocked on the door and entered.

"How is she, Doc?" Jack asked.

"Better," Dr. Benson answered. "The night nurse said last night was uneventful. I've taken her off the sedatives. She needs to wake up and eat to regain her strength. And if she keeps improving, she can be moved to the ward."

"Mama?" Camila asked in a weakened voice. She opened her eyes and asked, "Where is my mama?"

Dr. Benson looked at Jack with concern and empathy. Then he took the little girl's hand and told her, "Um, she's not here now. I'm Dr. Benson. I'm going to take care of you. What's your name, darling?"

"My name is Camila. Where's my mama? Where's Mateo?" she kept asking.

The doctor patted her on the head and told her, "Don't worry about them. You have to worry about getting better. That's why you're here. Understand? Just lie back and try not to move too much. We don't want your stitches to pop."

Camila turned her head toward the door and noticed Jack. "Who are you?"

Jack smiled and stepped forward. "My name's Jack. I'm a policeman," he said as he dug out his badge again to show it to her. "I was the one who found you in the closet. I'm here to protect you…to stop anybody from hurting you again."

"I…I don't remember," Camila answered groggily.

"That's OK, kid," said Jack. He reached into his coat again and asked, "Hey, can I show you something?"

"Detective…" warned the doctor curtly.

"Just a photo, Doc. That's all…" Jack walked up to the bed and showed the girl the picture of William and his wife holding hands.

"Camila, have you seen this man before?" asked Jack as politely as he could.

Camila looked at the smiling man in the photo. Then, the smiling image of William turned its head to look straight at the child. He dropped the smile and looked sternly at Camila. A knife appeared in his hand, and the image of William started jabbing the blade toward the girl.

Camila's eyes grew wide. She wanted to scream but was too overcome by terror. Summoning the rest of her strength, she finally managed to release a blood-curdling howl from the depths of her chest.

"The man! The MAN!" Camila yelled, pointing at William's photo. The image of him had transformed into a monstrous thing, laughing and pointing at her with glee at his ability to frighten the child. It seemed to gain strength from her panic. The menace of the photo finally overcame Camila, and, with a final scream, she collapsed into unconsciousness.

An infuriated Dr. Benson screamed at the detective, "I told you she was too weak and on drugs. There's no telling what she saw!"

Jack turned the photo around and saw William sitting with his wife. No change.

"I'm sorry, Doc. I didn't think she'd react that way," Jack said contritely.

"Get out!" commanded the doctor.

Jack started to back out of the hospital room and added as he reached the door, "Again, sorry. I hope she's OK…"

"She will be once you leave," said Dr. Benson. "Now, go!"

Jack obeyed. As he walked down the hall, he didn't feel the need to stay any longer. He'd been told what he needed to hear.

*

Jack made a stop at the communal coffee pot behind the front Precinct Nine desk. He was running on fumes as he drank the hot coffee as fast as his nerve endings in his mouth would allow. He refilled the cup and headed back toward the jail cells.

"Mornin', Nate," Jack said as he reached William's cell. William had been placed on suicide watch. Which meant Nate was stationed in a chair in front of the cell door.

"You look shitty, Detective," the jailer said. "Don't you get any sleep when you clock out?"

"We detectives never clock out," Jack answered, swigging his coffee. "How's this one doing?"

"He had a bad night," Nate said. "He was thrashing about so much that the doc was called in to knock him out. He's heavily sedated. Oh, and the doc said he needs to talk to you."

"Okay, thanks," Jack said. He realized he wasn't going to talk to William this morning. So, he turned to leave to see the doctor. He then stopped to tell Nate one last thing.

"By the way, when and if he rouses up, tell him he was wrong this time. He didn't kill both of the kids. The little girl survived," said Jack.

The detective turned to leave once more. But he was stopped in his tracks by the voice coming from inside the cell.

"I know," said William.

"Son of a bitch, I knew he'd say that…" Jack said, under his breath.

Kelly Key

CHAPTER 8

Dr. Gordon's clinic/dispensary was located on the floor above the jail cells to allow quick and easy access to the inmates. As Jack climbed the stairs to the doctor's office, he wondered if the physician had committed some form of malpractice to wind up being a doctor above a jail. Surely, having his own practice would be more lucrative. Jack made a point of not using him for medical assistance. He preferred making the trip to Clementine's doctor/boss instead.

Jack noticed the doctor's clinic door was ajar. Even though he was expected, the detective knocked anyway before going into the room.

"Hey, Doc, you here?" asked Jack as he looked around the small clinic. It contained one examining table, a sink, and shelves full of bandages and drugs that were safe to keep out in the open and not under lock and key.

"In here, Detective," answered Dr. Gordon from his adjacent office. He was sitting behind his desk, which was piled with books in every corner.

"The jailer said you wanted to talk to me?" Jack asked.

The doctor motioned for Jack to sit in the chair in front of his messy desk.

"I wanted to discuss what you know about Mr. Arbogast. He's quite disturbed," Dr. Gordon began.

Jack laughed nervously, "Yeah, tell me something I don't know."

"I've not administered any more sedatives to him," Gordon continued. "So, what's in his system should be wearing off soon. I wanted you to be there when I examine him."

"Sure…Okay…" Jack answered warily, not seeing why his presence was needed.

Gordon read Jack's face and explained, "You seem to have a connection with Mr. Arbogast…a calming effect, if you will. Before I could sedate him, he kept calling your name."

Jack ran his hand over his face in frustration and exhaustion from all things William. "Yeah, he does that. Lucky me."

"I want to ask him some questions while he's still groggy. We might find out more of the truth out of him if he's not in his fully conscious mind," said Gordon.

"Doc, I'm willing to help any way I can. But you're probably going to get the same story that he's told me when he's stone-cold sober," Jack said. "He thinks he's been killing these people when there's no way in the world he could've. Hell, I'm one of his alibis!"

"Is that so?" Gordon asked.

"Unfortunately, or fortunately, yes. The man knows all about these murders. He's got to have somebody on the outside doing them," said Jack.

The doctor stood and walked around his desk, looking at his watch. "Then perhaps what Mr. Arbogast says in a few minutes will help with your cases. Let's get down there."

*

When they entered William's cell, Jack and Dr. Gordon found him curled up in a ball. William was snoring and, in between the long snorts, seemed to be mouthing words.

"Come on, let's sit him up," said Dr. Gordon.

Jack took hold of one arm, and the doctor took hold of the other. They pulled William to the edge of his cot and sat him up. William slumped forward. Jack and the doctor had to hold him up, or he would've wound up in a ball on the cell's floor. When they pulled him up to a proper sitting position, William's head tossed back. He was still moving his lips but making no sound.

"Arbogast? Can you hear me?" asked the doctor.

"William? It's Jack. I'm here. Can you answer us?" Jack said in William's ear.

91

"I'm not William…" Arbogast whispered.

Jack shot a confused look at the doctor. He asked, "Is it the drugs talking?"

"That's why we're here…to find out," the doctor answered.

"Release me from this potion!" Arbogast said in a more potent whisper.

"You'll be awake soon, Arbogast. Are you able to answer some questions for us?" Gordon asked.

"Address me as Mr. Mallory," said Arbogast.

This made Jack cock his head to the side, like a dog hearing a high-pitched whistle. He shook William's body to see if that would rouse him to a more conscious state.

"Mallory? You're not making sense, William. Who are you talking about?" Jack asked as he continued to shake William's shoulders.

William slowly opened his eyes. He had a look of confusion on his face. He was discombobulated as to where he was. He looked around the room to get a sense of his location. He first looked at the doctor and then at Jack. He had to squint to focus on his face to finally recognize him.

"Detective Banks?" William began groggily. "What are you doing holding me like that? Have I been asleep?"

"William? Is that you?" Jack asked.

"Why, certainly, it's me," William answered. "I'm just a little tired, that's all…"

"Well, a minute ago, you wanted me to call you Mr. Mallory," Jack said.

William's eyes went from a squint to wide open upon the mention of that name. In a panic, he drew away from the detective, scooting across the bed to sit against the cell wall.

"How did you know that name?" asked William.

Jack shook his head, "I just told you. A minute ago, you wanted us to call you Mallory. That's all I know about the name."

William took a deep breath. He shook his head to come out of his drug-addled haze and be more focused before beginning his explanation.

"Fullerton Mallory was my business partner at the accounting firm. Or I should say I was his partner. He had started the firm and took me on as a staff accountant. A few years later, he made me his partner. We were a good match. He handled the business side—talking to clients, and I managed the accounts. The firm was small, but successful."

Jack stood up and began to pace. It was a habit that helped him think when he was questioning someone.

"William, you said that Mallory was your business partner. What happened to him?"

"Fullerton was murdered," William sighed in sorrow.

"Why?" asked Jack, still pacing, but maintaining eye contact with William.

"I've jumped to the end of the story," William continued. "Like I said, the firm was doing well. Then, something happened to Fullerton. His disposition changed overnight. He was never what I would call jovial. But he stayed in a good mood most days. Then he started getting mad all the time. Anything I or our staff did was wrong in his eyes. He began to yell and scream over petty things. He would never tell us why he was furious and short-tempered, nor could we appease or pacify him. He made work almost unbearable."

"You said he was murdered? By someone on the staff?" Jack asked.

William finally smiled. "No. But I'm sure some wanted to. We had a client who wouldn't pay us for our work. He was a retired general: General Moseby, who had served in the Civil War. He wasn't too deep in debt to us. But given Fullerton's new dark attitudes, he was not having it. Since he ran the business side, he was going to make sure the general paid us what was due. He went over to the general's house to collect. There was a heated argument, and, from General Moseby's account, Fullerton attacked him. The general pushed him off and grabbed one of his old swords to defend himself. Mallory wouldn't retreat, and so Moseby ran him through. But not before hacking him to pieces. He sliced through and cut off Fullerton's hands to make him stop attacking him."

"His hands? That's interesting," Jack commented.

"So, what?" asked Dr. Gordon. "What's so important about hands?"

"At every murder scene I've been to, the hands are in a particular position. Like they're special… enshrined, you might say."

"Mallory was buried with his severed hands crossed over his heart," William added.

"You seem to be around a lot of people who get hacked to pieces, William," Jack commented. He threw up his hands and said, "So, Mallory's dead. This is a dead end, William. Mallory can't be your killer. So, we're back where we started. But thanks for the story, William."

Dr. Gordon had sat there listening to the whole exchange between the prisoner and the detective. Now he wanted to ask some questions.

"All of this is well and good, Arbogast. But it doesn't explain why you wanted us to call you Mallory," said the doctor. "Why did you tell us to do so?"

William shrugged his shoulders, "Fullerton and I were very close. My late wife used to tease me that he was my second wife. Perhaps the drugs..."

"Hold on," Jack interrupted. "When did Mallory die?"

"A couple of months ago," William answered.

"And when did your wife and baby die?" Jack asked.

William dropped his head in sorrow, "Three weeks ago..."

"Jesus..." commented Dr. Gordon in sympathy. "And when did these visions you're experiencing begin?"

William had to gather himself for a moment. The wounds of his family's death were still fresh. He took a deep sigh and began, "Soon after Fullerton was killed, I started having bad dreams—flashes, really, of gruesome scenes. Scenes of sacrificial rituals, of animals being offered up to ancient gods, and sliced apart alive. There was gore and blood-drinking. I discounted them as dreams associated with the trauma of how Fullerton was killed. Then, they got worse..."

"When William?" Jack asked as he kneeled in front of him, still trying to maintain eye contact as a tool of trust.

"When I was left alone. After my wife and child...died..." William's words trailed off into sobs. "Tragic deaths...taken too soon!"

William shook his head and attempted to wipe his tears with his shoulders. His back heaved from the depth of his cries.

Jack stood up and placed his hands on William's head and shoulder. "I'm sorry, William. Thank you for the info. I think we're done here, Doc."

Jack tilted his head and nodded towards the cell door, indicating he wanted to talk to Dr. Gordon away from William. The doctor rose and turned to William, still crying on his bed.

"Get some rest, Mr. Arbogast," said the doctor. "I'll come and check on you later in the day."

*

Jack gripped Dr. Gordon's arm and led him out of the earshot of William's cell. When he felt he was far enough away, he stopped.

"Well, what about it, Doc?" asked Jack.

The doctor sighed and looked back toward William's cell, then back to the detective. "Arbogast's wounds aren't physical, Detective. They're emotional. As a physician, there's nothing I can really do for him other than to keep him sedated. And ethically, I can't keep administering sedatives to a mentally ill patient. It's really not my call. This man needs psychiatric help."

"That's a given, Doc," Jack said. "I think that's the next step. I just hate to see William committed to the loony bin. And if they keep him knocked out all the time, there goes my only connection to these murders."

"Did you hear anything from Arbogast that gives any clue today?" Dr. Gordon asked.

"Not much," Jack answered. "Him responding as Mallory may be something. It may have been the drugs, or it may have been his grief. But something's up with that…"

"I have a couple of psychiatrists in mind…" the doctor began.

"With all due respect, Doctor, I have a connection in the medical field who might know somebody. I'd like to try that road first," said Jack. His distrust of the doctor's circle of colleagues continued. If Gordon was practicing in a precinct jailhouse, where did his contacts work? And how proficient were they?

"Well, suit yourself," Dr. Gordon said. He started walking toward the stairs to his office and added, "You know where to find me."

*

Jack opened the door to Clementine's doctor's office. He would usually visit before or after hours, when the office was empty and quiet. He was surprised by how many people were packed into the front room, awaiting their assigned appointments. He scanned the sick and injured in the room. He saw minor cuts and nosebleeds, patients coughing and wiping their brows with sweat from fever.

Jack's visit had two missions. First, it was a good excuse to see his wife. And second, he had hoped the doctor could recommend a good psychiatrist to examine William. He walked over to the nurses' desk and stood there, waiting for his wife.

Clementine emerged from the doorway that led to the hallway of examining rooms. She was escorting a patient while giving him instructions about his medication.

"And remember, take this at a meal, or it will make you…Jack?" said a confused Clementine.

"What does that mean?" asked the patient, who was also confused.

Clementine turned to the patient. "I'm sorry. I meant to say: eat something with this, or you'll get sick. We have you coming back next Tuesday at ten for a follow-up," she continued, writing the date and time on a reminder card. She handed the card to the patient and added, "I hope you get better. See you next week."

She patted the man's shoulder and left him for Jack. "What are you doing here?"

"Hello, yourself," Jack answered. He put his arm around her waist, "I had a hankering for me some Clem stew."

"God, that's awful," Clementine critiqued and removed his arm. "You sort of caught me at a bad time, honey. We're covered up today."

"I can see that," he said. "Is it always this busy?"

"Only when we're open. Now, not to be short, what is it?"

"I'll get out of your hair real quick. I just need to ask the doctor something," he explained.

That made Clementine laugh, "Jack, if I'm busy, he's really busy. Can't it wait till tonight?"

Jack shook his head. "Tonight might be too late..."

"Too late for what?" Dr. Aderman interrupted. He had emerged from the examination rooms to look for Clementine.

An embarrassed Clementine answered, "I'm sorry, Doctor. You remember my husband, Jack?"

"Oh, yes. Your detective," Aderman joked. "Tell me, Jack, what's so important that you have to interrupt our patient flow?"

"I just need a name, Doc. I have a prisoner whose mind has gone bye-bye. He's my only connection to a series of murders. I need a great psychiatrist. All I need's a name, and I'll get out of your hair."

Dr. Aderman looked at Clementine. She looked back with her big brown eyes to plead her husband's case. The doctor let out a frustrated sigh and took a reminder card from her hand. He wrote a name and address on the back and handed it to Jack.

"I'm only doing this because your wife's the best damn nurse in here. He's one of the best at dealing with criminal types. I'd be surprised if the city will be able to afford him."

"All I can do is ask. Thanks, Doc!" Jack slipped the card into his coat pocket.

"Now kiss your wife and let us get back to work!" Dr. Aderman said as he turned toward the exam rooms' hallway door.

"Thanks again, Doc!" said Jack.

"Thank you, Doctor!" Clementine added.

The doctor waved dismissively and kept walking toward the door. Without turning around, he added, "And Clemmie, when you're finished smooching, bring back the next patient..."

CHAPTER 9

DR. HAROLD BANISTER

11 DOWNING WAY

Jack had to squint at Clementine's boss's handwriting to make it legible. After a subway ride from his precinct, he found Downing Way to be populated with medical offices. All of them had plaques or signs at their doors signaling which physician practiced there. He found 11 Downing Way and read the engraved plaque.

DR. HAROLD BANISTER, M.D.

PSYCHIATRIST/ALIENIST

"I hope you're in, Doc…" Jack whispered as he opened the door to the office.

The unlocked door was a good sign that, at least, someone was there. As Jack scanned the front room, he noticed how immaculate it was. Nothing seemed to be out of place. The pens and files on the desk in front of him were neatly arranged, as if each item had its assigned place and was returned there after use.

Jack noticed a bell at the front of the desk. It was the type used in hotels to ring for service. Jack tapped the button on top, and in the silent office, it rang with a loud, sharp "TING!"

"Who's there?" a voice asked from behind a closed office door.

"My name's Detective Jack Banks," yelled Jack. "I'm looking to talk to Dr. Banister?"

"I'm not seeing patients today," the voice replied. "Make an appointment with my secretary for later this week."

Jack looked down at the empty chair behind the front desk and yelled out, "Kinda hard to make an appointment with no secretary!"

Jack heard rustling behind the door and heard what he thought was muffled cursing. Then, a click of a lock and the door opened. There stood a middle-aged man with grey temples. He was nattily dressed in a brown woolen three-piece suit. To Jack, he seemed frustrated and confused at the same time. This was Dr. Harold Banister.

"Terribly sorry," he began. Jack immediately picked up on his English accent. "Edna must have stepped out. When do you want to come back?" he asked while opening the appointment book.

"Dr. Banister?" Jack asked. "Look, I don't want to come back. I'm not trying to be your patient. I'm here to ask you for help with a prisoner of mine."

"Police business?" he asked.

"Yes. It concerns several murders that have been taking place," Jack responded. "I've got a guy who 'sees' the murders as they happen. But there's no way he could have committed them. I think these visions have driven him insane."

Banister held up his hand to stop Jack from continuing. "Detective...?" He had not heard Jack's name through the closed door.

"Banks, Doctor. I'm Detective Jack Banks from the Ninth Precinct," Jack answered. This doctor was so proper that he felt compelled to show his badge to him. He then reached into his pocket to show Banister the appointment card with scribbles. "Dr. Aderman gave me your name."

"Aderman..." the doctor nodded in recognition. "Well, Detective Banks, whatever he told you I do, it's incorrect. I work with crime victims, the people scarred by the monsters you hopefully catch. I don't work on police cases, as such."

They both stood in silence for a minute. Believing that they were at an impasse. Jack stared at the floor, attempting to come up with any excuse to sway the psychiatrist.

"Believe me, Doctor, William Arbogast is the most tormented person I have ever dealt with. We have to keep him sedated to prevent him from killing himself."

"Sounds to me that this 'Arbogast' fellow belongs in an institution," the doctor commented. He stuck out his right hand, took Jack's hand, and shook it vigorously. "Now, thank you for coming, Detective. I'd like to talk longer, but I have a paper that's due. Terribly sorry I couldn't be more helpful. Please give my regards to Aderman. I will certainly set him straight the next time I run into him. If you'll show yourself out."

Banister let go of Jack's hand and gestured toward the front door. He then turned around to head back to his office.

Jack quickly placed his hand on the doctor's shoulder to stop him. The doctor froze in his tracks, shocked by the detective's audacity.

"It would be wise to remove your hand from my person, Detective!" Banister said sternly. He spun around to face Jack. The detective was successful in getting the doctor to stop.

"Sorry, Doc..." Jack began.

"Doc?" Banister asked in shocked revulsion. By his tone, Jack could tell immediately that Banister was accustomed to respect for his degree and not nicknames.

"Um, Doctor. Again, sorry..." Jack raised his hands in front of the psychiatrist and took a step back.

"You come into my office, interrupt my time, and then have the gall to treat me with such…familiarities!" he said, pulling his jacket down to straighten it. He then pulled a handkerchief from his pocket to wipe the spittle off his mouth.

Jack tried his best to calm the situation by saying, "Yeah, yeah. I'm awful. I didn't mean to upset you. If you'd just come and look at him…he's my only connection to four or more gruesome killings. He's getting worse. Hell, he's driving me crazy!" Jack said as he ran his fingers through his hair in frustration.

"Well, when he does drive you mad, you can make an appointment," Banister said with sarcasm.

"I deserved that. William's at the point that he thinks his old partner is living within him…" said Jack.

"What?" Banister asked, as his eyes widened in curiosity.

"He wanted us to call him Mallory, not Arbogast," Jack answered. "Mallory was killed a few weeks ago."

Dr. Banister put his hands behind him and started to pace in front of Jack. "Do you know what an alienist is, Detective?"

"I saw on the sign outside that you are one," Jack answered. "That's about it."

"Yes, quite," Banister said. "An alienist is an older term for a psychiatrist. Its use is fading in our vernacular. But it means someone who treats the mentally ill. I'm old enough to have been trained as an alienist before I earned my doctorate in psychiatry."

"Is there a difference?" Jack asked. He encouraged the doctor to continue. As long as the psychiatrist was talking, Jack was still in the room, looking for a chance to change his mind.

"The term alienist comes from the French *alieniste*. There used to be theories that mental illness was caused by something or someone 'alienating' a patient from their sanity. Something that causes a separation from reality."

"Well, I think you're right about the 'something' making William see these murders," commented Jack. "Here's the kicker…Doctor, I have witnesses who swear he was there at the murders. That he was actually the one who did the killings. I know for a fact otherwise."

"Psychic projection?" the doctor scoffed. "Impossible. You're entering into carnival sideshow talk. Parlor tricks to placate desperate rubes."

"Call it what you will, Dr. Banister, but these are the facts as I know them. People are being cut into pieces of meat. William's in a state of complete insanity. He needs your help. Hell, Banister, I need your help! Please, will you see him?" pleaded Jack.

"There you go, being rude again," the doctor pointedly said. He started pacing again, "Before I came to the States, I had been studying the theories of some of my colleagues in Europe about how the mind could be split into two or more people. Their personalities could be completely different. Nothing concrete yet. Perhaps this Arbogast took on the personality of…what did you say the name was?"

"Mallory," answered Jack.

"Yes, thank you. Perhaps Arbogast, after Mallory's death, adopted that personality to keep him 'alive,' as it were, out of some guilt or even a type of mourning."

"Sounds like a theory," Jack said in encouragement. "William told me they were close. Good research candidate, Doctor?"

Banister huffed in frustration and resignation. He walked over to the appointment book and turned the page to the next day's time slots. He ran his finger down the page to find an opening.

"I will see him tomorrow morning at eight sharp. Have him ready and in an office. I will not examine him in a jail cell," the doctor commanded.

Jack broke out a smile, "Anything you say, Doctor Banister. Ninth Precinct House. Eight o'clock sharp. I'll have him awake and ready. And I'll tell them you're coming."

"I hope this isn't a waste of my time," said the doctor.

"Thanks. I'll see you there!" Jack said. He left the office and, on the front step, ran into a woman who was about to enter the building.

"Sorry, lady," said Jack, grabbing the woman's arm to prevent her from falling. "You must be Edna."

The woman stepped back in shock. "How did you know my name?"

Jack smiled, "I'm a detective!"

*

The next morning, Dr. Gordon led William, still strapped into a straitjacket, from his cell and into an office off the main room of the precinct house. William was still groggy from the drugs that had been administered to him. Dr. Gordon brought in a metal coffee pot. He poured the coffee into a cup and held it to William's mouth for him to drink, hoping that it would clear his mind.

*

Jack waited outside on the sidewalk for Dr. Banister. He made sure he was out there before eight o'clock, as Banister gave him the impression that he was impeccably prompt. He looked at his watch, then looked down the street. There was Banister, emerging from a horse-drawn cab. Jack waved at Banister to see him.

"Thanks for coming, Doctor," Jack told him. "William's inside."

"I've never been to this part of the city before. I believe I shan't be inclined to return," admitted the doctor as he scanned the run-down buildings and the precinct entrance in front of him.

They made their way to the office where William was being kept. As they entered the room, Jack introduced the doctors to each other.

"Dr. Gordon, this is Dr. Harold Banister, a psychiatrist," Jack began.

"And alienist," Banister added.

"Oh, yeah. Dr. Banister, Dr. Gordon, our staff medical doctor…" said Jack.

As Gordon approached Banister to shake his hand, Banister stopped him and said, "Dr.... Gordon is it?"

"Yes," answered Gordon.

"Please be a good chap and remove the straitjacket from the patient," commanded Dr. Banister.

"What?" asked a startled Gordon. "This 'patient' is suicidal! He's likely to harm himself and maybe us, too!"

"The patient needs to feel as comfortable as possible. It's part of my method," said Banister.

"The patient's name is William!" objected Arbogast.

"See! He's getting agitated!" Gordon protested.

"C'mon, Doc, I'll help with the jacket. I'll stay and make sure William doesn't do anything to himself," Jack said, trying to bring down the temperature in the room.

Dr. Gordon took a long pause, staring at Banister. The silence in the room was getting thicker and thicker. Each doctor was determined not to break it. A battle of wills and territories was brewing. There was rage in Gordon's eyes.

Then, Gordon turned to Jack and said bitterly through his teeth, "If the doctor wants the jacket off, he can remove it himself. I'm a doctor, not his orderly. If needed, I'll be in my infirmary..."

With that, Dr. Gordon picked up his medical bag and left the office. He opened the door wide and slammed it behind him.

Dr. Banister calmly watched him leave, and when Gordon was out of the room, he admitted, "Well. Pleasant fellow. He saved me the embarrassment of asking him to leave."

Jack went over to William to unbuckle the straitjacket. As he was helping William take it off, he said, "I hope nothing happens to you while you're here, Doctor. I'd hate for Dr. Gordon to treat you after that."

"Why did you wake me up?" William asked Jack as he reached for the coffee cup to take a deep drink. "Being drugged is the only time I get peace. I don't have any visions when I'm knocked out."

"Is that so?" Banister asked as he sat down across from William.

"William, this is Dr. Banister," Jack said, pointing his hand toward the doctor. "He's a psychiatrist. He's here to see if he can help you."

"Help me?" asked William. "A crazy doctor?"

"I assure you, Mister…Arbogast, is it? I am not crazy," Banister joked. "I have a degree in psychiatry and am an alienist. I have studied at several European universities. So, Mr. Arbogast, I know all about crazy. And I am not that."

"How can you help me stop killing people?" William asked.

"Well, from what the detective tells me, it's impossible that you killed these people," Banister declared.

"I'm there, Doctor. I see and hear it all. I cause and witness their fear and pain and anguish," William whispered.

"You say these are visions, authentic experiences to you. You actually feel like you're there?" asked Banister.

"I told you, Doctor, I'm there!" William was growing agitated with having to repeat everything.

"Right. Tell me, William, the sequence of your experiences. What happens right before they start?"

"Um, I'm asleep. There's a void...blackness. Then, the next thing I know, I'm there at the murder scene. It's like curtains being opened and I'm there."

"I see. So, it's like something or someone is presenting this to you. Showing you the place and people, and you act on it?"

"Yes, I suppose..." William answered.

"Would you say the something or someone who brings you there is making you murder these people?" asked Banister.

"I...I don't know..." William trailed off and stared into space, as if the doctor had hit a nerve and William didn't want to answer him.

"The Detective said at some point, you wanted to be called Mallory. What do you think, William, is the significance of that?"

"I...I was drugged. I don't remember saying that..." William trailed off again.

"Do you think that this Mallory fellow would be behind showing you your experiences?"

William quickly turned to Banister and asked, "Why would you think that? Mallory was my partner, my friend."

"Please don't get upset, William. I'm just trying to catch up, to understand your situation," Banister explained, trying to calm down the patient.

"I tell you I'm doing these things. Not Mallory," William said emphatically. "Mallory's dead and gone. God rest his soul."

"I see. Tell me, how do your 'experiences' end?" Banister asked, trying to get back on track.

"They don't end until I wake up," William replied.

"Do people talk to you in your experiences?"

"Yes."

"What do they say?"

"They expect me to arrive. Like I've already made plans with them. Then, later, they beg for their lives. It's horrible. I'm horrible," William uttered as he put his face in his hands.

"I see," said Banister. "Detective, you've been able to verify everything he tells you?"

"Yes," Jack answered. "He knows everything. Right down to the address and what room the bodies can be found."

Banister sighed to think for a minute. He nodded his head toward the door. He wanted to talk to Jack outside the office.

"William, I need to step out a moment with the detective. We'll be right on the other side of the door," explained the doctor.

Jack grabbed both of William's shoulders and made him look up. He said, "William, I'm trusting you to stay in your chair while I'm out. I'll be able to see you through the window in the door. So, no trying to end yourself, OK? We're trying everything we can to help you. Understand?"

"Alright," William agreed.

*

Dr. Banister and Jack went into the hall to confer. Jack never took his eyes off William. He watched him through the window of the office door.

"Did you notice?" Banister asked.

"Notice what?" asked Jack.

"Every time Mallory was brought up, Arbogast either tried to kill the conversation or said he didn't remember. He's hiding something. Are you sure this Mallory fellow is dead?'

"Yes, I checked yesterday after William told us he was killed. Like he said, about two months ago."

"Hmm," the doctor said. "I thought he might have been a figment of Arbogast's imagination. An alternate personality. Detective, if we can get Arbogast to agree, I'd like to try a different method."

Jack sighed, "Why not? Everything else has failed."

Kelly Key

CHAPTER 10

Jack and Dr. Banister opened the office door and found William bent over the table, resting his head on his folded arms. His head was turned away from the door. Banister sat down in the chair opposite William.

"William," Banister began, "I have a procedure that might give us more insight into what's going on inside your mind. It involves the use of a drug. With your permission, of course."

"Will it knock me out?" William asked, with his head still resting on his arms. "I want to be sedated."

"Eventually," Banister answered as he opened his medical bag. "But first, it will bring you to a state of what I can only describe as 'euphoria.' You won't care about anything. And maybe we can go deep into your mind to find some answers. Are you willing to try it?"

William raised his head and sat up in his chair. "As long as it knocks me out and gives me respite from this torment, I'm willing."

"Good. Please roll up your sleeve," Banister said.

"Doctor, do you mind me asking what you're about to give my only connection to those murders?" asked Jack. "I don't want his mind gone. I need him."

Dr. Banister smiled and explained as he prepared two syringes. "It's a natural extract called Scopolamine. It produces what is termed a 'twilight sleep.' The patient is conscious and unconscious at the same time. Along with a second drug, it removes one's guards and inhibitions. This makes the patient cooperative and more open to suggestion. And, not to worry, William will be his own cheerful self when it wears off."

Banister administered the injections to William and sat back in the chair. "Now we wait," he said as he replaced the vials of drugs in his medical bag. Over the next few minutes, he watched his subject's eyelids grow heavier and heavier. They eventually closed, and William's head rocked back to face the ceiling.

Jack stepped over to William and pushed the semi-conscious man's head over to where his chin was resting on his chest. Jack looked up at the psychiatrist and asked, "Well, what about it, Doctor?"

Banister took William's hand and raised his arm. He let the hand go, and William's arm limply fell to his side.

"Hmm…" said Banister. "I believe we're ready to start. William, can you hear me?"

William raised his chin from his chest. He stared blankly ahead, locking eyes with neither the doctor nor Jack. His half-opened eyes became slits.

"William's asleep. I watched you do that to him," said a whisper coming from William's mouth.

Banister and Jack looked at each other. Jack shook his head and shrugged his shoulders in uncertainty. Banister only raised an eyebrow in fascination and turned back to William.

"Yes, quite," the doctor affirmed. "Am I to understand that I am not speaking to William at this moment? If so, you have me at a disadvantage. With whom am I speaking? Are you Mr. Mallory?"

"I am Mallory," he whispered.

"Ah," replied the doctor. He glanced at Jack with a nod of verification. "Well, Mr. Mallory, I have it from very reliable sources that you recently died. Why are you still here?"

"He keeps me here," he whispered.

Banister nodded, "You mean William? Shouldn't he let you go?" The psychiatrist was attempting to suggest as much to William during this state of "twilight." He thought that William would perhaps understand and shrug off this burden of an extra personality.

"It's not William," said the whisper. "He keeps me prisoner to watch."

"To watch…?" asked the doctor.

"To watch the killing. He is evil," he whispered.

"There is another?" Banister asked.

"I…I cannot tell. He won't let me," the whispers began to have a tremble of fear in them. "I only wanted to come forward to tell William. I brought this on him. And to apologize. I didn't know what I was dealing with. By the time I did, he had taken me over."

"I hate to be a nag, Mallory," said Banister. "But you cannot tell me who 'he' is?"

There was a long pause. Eventually, a soft whimper left William's mouth, followed by a low whisper, "It's not for me to say. He feeds on fear. He's feeding off me now!"

The whisperer let out a low moan and fell silent.

"Mallory? Mr. Mallory? Are you still talking to us?" the psychiatrist asked.

"William?" asked Jack. "William! There's nothing to fear. You're here with me and the doctor. Nobody else. William?!"

William's eyes closed completely. He wasn't asleep. He was unconscious, completely knocked out.

"Is he OK?" asked Jack with concern.

Banister sighed, "I'm afraid the Scopolamine has overtaken him for the moment."

The doctor rose from the chair and began to pace in front of Jack. He continued, "At least three persons who reside in Arbogast's mind. A fascinating case, indeed. Thank you, Detective, for bringing him to my attention."

"Well, glad I could help, Doctor," Jack said sarcastically. "But remember, you're here to help me. And to tell ya the God's honest truth, I'm not feeling helped. He said nothing that would point me toward who the real killer is."

"Sorry, I didn't have enough time to get around Mallory before Arbogast passed out," the doctor explained. "There was that one thing about 'feeding on fear.' When Mallory's voice was talking about it, he sounded genuinely frightened. I've never experienced a subject like this. One personality dominating another."

"All well and good, Doctor," said Jack, throwing up his hands in frustration. "All this tells me is Mallory's not the killer. And I already knew that because he's dead!"

"I would ask you to lower your voice, sir," Banister uttered defensively. "You wanted me to help this man and you. You have a poor way of showing gratitude."

"I'll show gratitude when I find who's killing these people," Jack shot back.

"I killed them," said a voice out of William's mouth. It was a low and menacing growl. It didn't sound like the whine of William at all.

"William?" asked Jack. "You're back?"

119

"Do you think I'm William? It wouldn't be the first time you thought I was him," said the voice.

Banister dropped his hostility toward Jack and sat back down in the chair opposite William.

"If you're not William, who are you?" Banister asked.

William's eyes stared straight at the doctor. "Another physician, another concoction. Stop filling this body with your potions."

"Why?" asked Jack.

"You're hindering me. But I'll find a way out. I always do," replied the voice.

"Are you going to tell us who you are?" asked Banister.

"I go by many names," answered the voice. "It depends on your religion and where you come from."

The doctor looked at Jack with both brows raised. He went back to William's body and replied, "Religion, eh? Well, I was raised in the Church of England. What would I know you as?"

The voice shook William's head, "I can tell you haven't practiced your faith in many years. A fallen man. You wouldn't recognize my Christian name."

"Right. We could do this all day. Should I call you Coy? Because that's how you're acting," Banister replied. He thought confrontation might provoke anger, and riling up this personality might yield answers.

"For your satisfaction, you can call me Gray," the voice answered. "I like gray because it is so plain and enigmatic. It keeps you guessing."

"Well... 'Gray,'" Jack said sarcastically. "You claim to have killed these people if you're inside William's mind?"

"I come and go as I please. You've seen me, Jack," he said in a condescending tone. "I was the one outside your bedroom window, watching you make love to your fetching wife."

Jack's hand balled up into a fist. He was about to punch William. Luckily, the doctor saw his rage. He managed to grab the detective's fist and hold it down at Jack's side.

"He's already semiconscious, Detective. Making him unconscious won't help either of us," Banister said. "Is what he's saying true?"

"There was a man looking in our bedroom window from the fire escape," Jack said. "But William would know that because I accused him of being that man."

"I see," Banister said. He then turned back his attention to the voice. "Mister...Gray, is it? You want us to sit here and believe you can leave Mister Arbogast's body and murder at will?"

"Believe what you will," said the voice. "I would prove it to you if not for the potion. I'll soon find a way out. I need to feed."

"Mallory said you feed on fear?" Jack asked.

"Mallory talks too much. I will drain him so that he won't talk again. Fear is the ultimate controller. Fear gives me power. Fear is why I show William he's murdering those lost souls. William makes a good host. He also makes a good alibi. He can't be in two places at once, can he?"

"Is that why you torment him?" Jack asked. "To suck the life out of him?"

"This host is overflowing with fear. But he'll soon be gone. I'll have to find another host. You see, fear is everywhere, Detective," said the voice. Then William's face smiled as the voice said, "And as soon as I escape, fear will be at 24 Andover Lane."

This time, Banister couldn't hold Jack's hand back. With lightning speed, Jack delivered a rugged right cross to William's smiling face. He followed that with several more punches to his face and head until William was knocked out.

"Detective! Now we won't find any more answers!" protested Banister.

"Put him out, Doc!" Jack ordered Banister. He was so enraged that he'd forgotten that the doctor loathed that nickname. "Put him so far under that he won't wake up for days!"

"Do you mind letting me know what set you off so?" asked the psychiatrist as he started to fumble with his medicine bag.

"The address," Jack said. "It's where my wife is staying with her mother."

Jack grabbed his coat and opened the office door. "Jailer! Tell Dr. Gordon we're done. Get this slug back to his cell."

"Wait. Are you leaving?" asked a shocked Banister.

"I'm going to get my wife. Thanks for coming, Doc!" Jack took one last look at William and ran down the hall.

"What?" asked Banister, yelling at Jack from the office door. "You don't actually believe in that spiritual rubbish he was spewing, do you?"

Jack turned around but kept his fast pace to respond, "If you'd seen what I've been seeing, you'd be more inclined to believe something's going on! Let's just say I have an open mind. I gotta go."

Jack burst through the front doors of the precinct house and raced down the street. All along the way, he thought about Clementine and what he might have brought upon her. He had to make sure that she was alright.

*

Clementine was already at work that morning, signing patients in for their appointments with Dr. Aderman. She was sitting at her desk when Jack swung open the office door.

"Jack?" Clemmie said. Then she saw the look of concern on his face. "What's wrong?"

"We have to go," said Jack as he took her arm and lifted her from the chair.

"What?" she asked, jerking her arm from his hand. "I can't leave. We have patients..."

"Clemmie, you and your mother might be targets. I have to get you to a safe place," Jack explained. "Now, get another nurse up here and I'll square it with Aderman later."

Clementine took a beat and called down the hall, "Vernie, can you cover the front desk? Something's come up and I have an emergency!"

The nurse, Lavergne, came running from the examination rooms. "What's the matter, Clemmie?"

"Hopefully nothing," Jack replied. "But I can't take any chances. Hate to leave you in a lurch. Apologies to Dr. Aderman. Let's go, Clemmie."

Clemmie looked at Lavergne and shrugged her shoulders. After mouthing, "Sorry" to her, she left with Jack, barely able to keep up with his fast pace. She caught up to him and slapped him on the arm. Jack never broke his stride.

"Alright, Jack. It's time for an explanation," demanded an irate Clemmie. She was tired of all the vagueness.

"Aderman's psychiatrist friend drugged William. He threatened to kill you and your mother," Jack explained.

"Well, he can't do that from jail," said Clemmie.

"He's already been associated with deaths from there. He knew your mother's address," Jack answered. He stopped on the sidewalk and grabbed Clemmie by the shoulders. "When it comes to you, I don't want to take any chances." He then hugged his wife hard.

Jack's hug thoroughly convinced Clemmie that the situation was dire enough to cause concern. She separated from Jack and nodded, "Let's go get Mother."

*

They reached the apartment building on Andover Lane and rushed up the stairs to the second-floor apartment. Jack tried the door, and it was locked. Clemmie immediately started digging through her purse for the key.

The door opened, and there stood Clemmie's mother, Gladys. Her careworn face looked bewildered.

"Jack? Clem?" she asked. "What in the world…"

By this time, Jack was tired of explaining William to people. "Long story short, Mrs. Fallon, one of my prisoners threatened to kill you and Clemmie. I need to get you two to a safe place."

"What? Why?" Gladys asked as Jack and Clemmie hurried past her to enter the apartment.

"I'll explain later, Mother," answered Clemmie. "We need to trust Jack and get out of here for a few days."

"Are we in danger?" she asked.

"Yes," Jack and Clemmie said simultaneously.

Both Clementine and her mother packed their suitcases for a week's stay. Where they were going, neither knew. The three left the apartment, with Clementine locking the door behind them.

As they descended the stairs, Jack was behind the two women. When they reached the landing on the first floor, Jack saw a figure in the hallway. Standing 10 feet away was William. Jack had to blink twice to make sure.

"Clem, take your mother down to the street. I have to talk to this man," Jack said.

"What?" asked Clementine.

"Please just do it. I'll be down in a minute," Jack demanded.

The figure of William took a step forward. This prompted Jack to draw his gun from under his coat.

"Hi, 'Jack,'" said the figure. He used the detective's name sarcastically, mockingly.

"William?" Jack asked. He still couldn't believe his eyes. William couldn't possibly be there.

"No, Jack," said the figure. "Guess again. Clem's mother has a nice place…"

"If you try to harm my family, I'll kill you, William!" Jack yelled. He pointed the gun at the figure.

The figure laughed at Jack and shook his head as he explained condescendingly, "William's not here, Jack. William's in jail. You can't shoot a shadow."

Jack decided to try anyway. He fired two shots at the figure. The bullets hit the wall behind the figure of William, appearing to whiz right through it. This made the figure laugh.

"I told you I'd find a way out, Jack. I always do!" Then, the figure smiled and faded from Jack's sight.

Jack thought the best thing to do was to get his family out of there. He ran down the stairs to join Clemmie and her mother, who were waiting on the sidewalk.

CHAPTER 11

Jack rushed out of the door to the apartment building on Andover Lane. Clementine saw him emerge and ran over to him.

"Did I hear gunshots?" she asked. "Are you alright?"

"I'm fine. I had a little run-in with the killer," Jack answered.

"You mean William? Did you get him?" Clemmie asked. She had a confused look on her face.

"No, it wasn't William. And I didn't," Jack replied. "C'mon, we have to go. And fast."

Jack put his arm around Clementine's waist and pushed her along to where her mother was standing. Her mother picked up her suitcase and joined them.

"Where are we going?" Gladys asked.

"I'm taking you back to the precinct house," said Jack.

Clementine wrestled herself away from Jack's arm and stopped on the sidewalk. A look of dread flashed across her face. She asked, "You mean where William is? You're putting us in the same building as the killer? Are you nuts?"

Jack stopped, too, and shook his head. "William's not the killer. I'm convinced of that now. He's no more than an alibi for the real killer. A receptacle."

"Receptacle?" Clemmie asked. "What does that mean?"

Jack reached for Clementine's hand. He then continued walking with her at his side.

"After all this is over, I'll set you two down and try my best to explain it to you…if I can. Right now, let's get to the precinct house. I'll grab a couple of beds from the back and set you two up in an office. It'll be cramped. But it'll be safe," said Jack.

"I still won't feel safe when I'm that close to William," Clemmie commented. "Who knows when and where that killer will strike. But William will know."

"Look, if there's one thing I've figured out about this murderer, it's that it likes to kill when someone's alone. It pumps up the fear…which it likes. And believe me, Clem, you'll never be alone at Precinct Nine. There are men with guns there twenty-four-seven," Jack said.

"How long is this going to be?" asked the mother.

"A day? A week?" answered Jack. "All I know is that it needs to kill again."

"Needs to?" asked Clemmie.

"It told me it feeds on fear," Jack explained. "And it's been a couple of days since the last killing. It'll be looking for a victim, and soon. I need to catch it before it does."

"How?" Clemmie asked.

Jack lowered his head and answered, "I wish I knew…"

"You keep saying 'it'," Gladys observed.

"I sure do," was Jack's only answer.

*

As the detective escorted his family down the street, he wondered to himself what he had gotten himself into. He witnessed two bullets pass through the body of that thing, and they didn't harm it in the least.

He then began thinking about the entity and its statement that it fed on fear. To many, fear is a crippling thing. It makes people pause. And it makes people hesitate before acting. Fear makes people turn around and go the other way. Jack knew he couldn't do that. It was his job to face this thing and find a way to stop it, regardless of his fears.

He couldn't be afraid. He looked over at Clementine as they walked hand in hand down the street. He gave her a slight smile to make her feel better…hell, to make him feel better.

*

Edna arrived at Dr. Banister's office at 7:50 the next morning. She always wanted to arrive at the office a few minutes early to review the day's appointments and ensure the office was ready before officially opening at 8.

She unlocked the door and entered. She immediately noticed Banister's office door was ajar and the lamp was still on. A shaft of light shone through the cracked-open door, illuminating part of her desk.

"Another all-nighter…" Edna mumbled with a sigh and a shake of her head. Dr. Banister had a reputation for studying cases and writing papers long after the office had stopped seeing clients during the day. So, Edna didn't think twice that there might be something amiss.

She didn't hear the doctor stirring in the office. She continued to shake her head and said to herself, "Probably asleep at his desk again."

Edna put down her purse and removed her coat. As she hung the coat on the rack behind her desk, she called out, "Good morning, Doctor! Would you like some coffee? I'll be glad to make some!"

She heard no response from Banister. Surely, he didn't leave without turning out the light.

"Dr. Banister? Are you here?" she asked as she made her way to the door. "Dr.?"

Edna knocked on Banister's office door as was her custom before entering. She opened the door wider and saw the blood on the floor. Edna gasped and looked up at the desk. There was Banister's severed head sitting on top of the desk. Two pens had been stabbed in each of his eyes. Both held notes that were written in the doctor's blood. Both were addressed to Jack Banks.

Edna almost swooned and fainted at the gory sight. She composed herself enough to let out a shriek. She turned and ran out of the office, screaming.

*

Jack had explained his situation to Chief Dooley. He was careful to leave out the mystical paranormal elements of the story, as the chief might have considered him as loony as William. He had told him a man had threatened to kill Clementine and her mother, and that her place as well as his apartment were known to the killer.

He had found two extra beds in empty cells and moved them to an unoccupied office for Clemmie and her mother. Because the beds were single twin beds, Clemmie didn't get to sleep with her husband again. Jack would sleep next to his wife on top of the desk in the spare office.

"Everybody decent?" asked Chief Dooley from the other side of the office door.

Jack had been awake for hours on top of the desk when Dooley arrived at the door. All the thoughts in his head were focused on that thing that called itself "Gray." Jack heard the chief at the door and got up off the desk. He looked down at Clemmie and her mother, who were still asleep in the beds.

"One second, Chief," Jack whispered. He went to the door and opened it. Then he silently closed it behind him.

"I let you sleep in a little," said Dooley.

"I wasn't asleep. You could have come earlier," Jack muttered in a sleepy fog. "I have a lot to do and think about."

"We've got a report, Jack. It concerns that psychiatrist that you brought in yesterday," the chief began.

"Yeah? What about him?" Jack asked. He was groggy from lack of sleep and didn't make the connection that something might have happened to Banister.

"He's been murdered, Jack," Dooley said.

"What?" Jack finally snapped to consciousness from the shock of Banister's death.

"They found him in his office…in pieces," explained the chief.

"Aw, dammit!" Jack shouted. Realizing Clemmie was on the other side of the door, he motioned for his boss to move away from the office.

"There's more, Jack. The cops on the scene said there were two notes pinned to his head. Both were addressed to you. You better get down there," Dooley said.

"Did William say anything about it?" Jack asked.

"He's out cold. Whatever the doctor gave him must've packed a powerful wallop. They said he hasn't stirred since he was put down," replied the chief.

"Yeah. That makes sense," Jack commented, nodding his head.

"How so?" asked Dooley.

"William's not the problem anymore. I need to go. Tell Clemmie I got called out. But don't tell her it was Banister. I will when I get back."

"Alright," the chief agreed. "And for God's sake, will you keep me posted? Most of the time, I don't even know what's going on."

Jack shook his head, "That makes two of us, Chief. I'll get back as soon as I can."

*

When Jack arrived at Dr. Banister's office, he went up to the policeman posted at the door and pulled out his badge to gain entry.

"Detective Jack Banks," he told the officer. "I was working with the victim on a case."

"Alright," said the officer. The detective handling the case is inside, talking to the receptionist."

"Thanks," said Jack. He entered the office to find a detective interviewing Edna. He approached the two and showed them his badge.

"I'm Detective Jack Banks, from the Ninth Precinct," he said.

"Detective," the other detective acknowledged. "I'm Detective North. Mrs. Naismith was just telling me there were notes addressed to you on the victim's body."

"Edna," Jack began. Unlike Banister, he always made a point to remember the names of the people he'd met. "I just heard about this before coming over here. I'm sorry for your loss. I only worked with the doctor yesterday. He seemed to know his stuff."

"Dr. Banister could be short with people. But he had a good heart. He was only trying to help them as quickly as possible. I came across the pond to work for him. We liked and depended on each other. Now, I don't know what I'll do," said Edna. She sat down at her desk and put her head in her hands.

"I'm sorry, Edna," Jack said in the most comforting way he could muster. He patted her arm and looked at Detective North. "My chief told me about the notes. Where are they?"

"They're where we found them, on his desk," said North. "Mrs. Naismith, will you be alright while I show the detective into the other room?"

Edna nodded, "I'll stay here. Seeing the Doctor in that shape again would be too much."

"Thanks, we won't be long," said Jack.

Dr. Banister's office had not been disturbed by the policemen. It was precisely as Edna had discovered it. Banister's body parts were strewn all over the floor. His limbs had shredded ends. Jack realized Banister's arms and legs hadn't been cut off by a knife or saw. They had been torn off, ripped from their sockets.

Jack stepped up to the deck and muttered to Banister's severed head, "Sorry for getting you into this, Doctor. I thought we had him trapped."

Jack looked around the room for the telltale signature of all the murders. He didn't see them.

"Did you find the hands?" Jack asked.

"They're still attached to the arms," North answered in a confused manner. "Why? Is that important?"

Jack stepped around the desk and bent down to examine a severed arm that had been thrown under it. He picked up the torn-off arm, still clothed in Banister's bloody shirt sleeve. The hand was still in place.

"Goodbye, Mallory. I guess you're not around anymore. So, the hands weren't important to anybody else but you. I hope the doctor didn't take your place."

"Huh?" asked a confused Detective North.

"I've been investigating a series of murders. All the victims were dismembered by a knife or cleaver. Chopped to pieces. In every one of the cases, the hands were severed and placed in a certain position. Almost like a shrine—a taunt to a man that had his hands cut off," Jack explained while he folded his hands, one over the other, to demonstrate.

"Then, it might not be the same killer," said North.

"Oh, it's him, all right," Jack said as he pulled the pins holding the notes from the doctor's eye sockets. "This was a direct message to me."

Jack slid the bloody notes off the pins. *TO DETECTIVE JACK BANKS* was scratched out in the doctor's blood above the folds of both.

Jack opened the right one. It read:

DR. BANISTER WAS A NONBELIEVER. HE IS THAT NO MORE. I MADE HIM BELIEVE IN ME. HE WILL MAKE ME A GOOD COMPANION.

Then Jack read the second one:

FREE WILLIAM. OR YOU AND CLEMENTINE WILL JOIN BANISTER.

IF YOU DON'T KNOW FEAR, YOU SOON WILL...

Jack looked up from the note and whispered to himself an epiphany, "It's keeping Banister…"

"What did you say?" asked North.

"Hmm?" asked Jack. He jerked a little, like he was being shaken out of a brain fog. As he fumbled to refold the notes before the other detective could read them, he answered, "Oh, nothing. Do you mind if I keep these notes? They'll help in my investigation."

North tilted his head, not believing the detective would ask to take something from a murder scene. He put his hands on his hips and said, "Well, they're evidence for this murder…"

Jack shoved the notes in his coat pocket and made his way toward the door. "If you think about it, this murder is all part of my investigation. We're all one big team. Thanks for understanding, Detective!"

"Hey! Wait a minute!" protested Detective North. He tried catching up to Jack. But he was already out of the office and onto the street.

Jack was on a hard run. He needed to return to the precinct house as quickly as possible. He needed to get back to William.

*

The detective burst through the precinct doors and headed directly toward the jail cells. Clementine happened to be in the hall outside the office where the family had spent the night. She saw Jack coming at a fast pace.

"Where did you go off to, Jack?" asked Clemmie. "What's going on?"

"Jack stopped long enough to kiss his wife on the forehead. He then broke away and said, "Clem, I promise I'll be back in a minute to fill you in. I have to check on something first. I'll be right back."

Jack left Clemmie bewildered, standing in the hall. He hurried back to William's cell.

"Tommy!" Jack hollered to the jailer. "I need to see William! Bring the key!"

"Jesus!" exclaimed Tommy as he rushed toward the cell door and fumbled to find the right key. "What's all the hubbub?"

"I need to talk to William," Jack explained.

Tommy chuckled as he turned the lock, "Ha! Good luck with that! He's still sleeping off the drugs that the head doctor gave him yesterday."

"I've got to make him come to. At least halfway," Jack said as he entered the cell.

Jack found William curled up on his side in a fetal position. He faced the wall.

The detective rolled William over on his back. He grabbed the front of the straitjacket and started shaking the drugged man.

"Come on, William!" Jack yelled. "Wake up! Show me that Banister's in there!"

William let out a low moan. But showed no signs of waking.

Now frustrated, Jack slapped William's cheek and decided to take the direct approach. "Dr. Banister, can you hear me? Can you talk to me?"

William's eyes slowly opened, and he looked at Jack. Then a voice emerged: "Help me, detective!" it whispered.

"How, Banister?" Jack asked.

"Get a priest. It's a demon!" whispered the voice.

"What?' Jack asked in a shocked voice.

"I can say no more. It's returned! God help me!"

With that, the voice trailed off with a whimpering sob. William's eyes closed, and he returned to his drug-induced sleep.

CHAPTER 12

"Banister?" pleaded the detective. He grabbed the straitjacket's material and shook William's body. Then, in his anger, he demanded, "Banister! Talk to me! What priest?"

William's eyes jerked open to look at Jack. His face was contorted into a mask of evil. The wicked face broke out into a broad smile, and another voice from inside William said in a raspy whisper, "The doctor is mine now, as you will be soon! Then, you can talk to him all you want!"

As William shut his eyes and fell back into unconsciousness, Jack let go of the straitjacket and stepped back from William's bed. He realized that "Gray" had returned to William's body, and he wouldn't hear from Dr. Banister again. Shaken by the interaction with the two entities inside the body of William, the detective backed away from the bed and left the cell.

Making sure the jailer locked the cell door, Jack made his way out of the holding area and back into the hall. As soon as he shut the door, he fell backward and leaned on it. For the first time in a long time, Jack felt helpless. He had thought Dr. Banister held the solutions he needed to free William and get the information on how to catch the killer. Now, Banister was gone, and the killer had free rein to move about the world and kill on a whim.

None of Jack's skills or talents could figure out what to do next. He felt alone in the world. Then, Clementine emerged from the office down the hall. She turned and saw Jack. The look on her face was not one of love and devotion. It was one of lividness. She stomped down the hall toward her husband.

"Jack Banks! I've had enough of being kept in the dark. What in holy hell is going on? Where did you go without telling us?" she yelled as she came closer to stand one inch from the detective's face.

Jack's only answer was to grab Clemmie and hug her tightly. The embrace was so tight that Clemmie began to lose her breath. She struggled to loosen it.

Clemmie pushed against Jack's chest to separate enough to breathe. "What was that for, Jack? If you think affection is going to get you out of the way you've been acting, you're…"

"I'm sorry, Clem," Jack began with remorse in his voice. "I'm sorry for ever getting involved with this case. It's done nothing but put you in danger. I never wanted that."

"What?" asked Clemmie. "Jack, what are you talking about? Dammit, will you stop protecting me and let me in!"

"The killer has threatened to come after you if I don't do what it wants—to let William go. I don't know how to stop it," Jack said.

"Now you're talking crazy. You said yourself this guy can't get us in here," said Clemmie.

"It's not a man, Clemmie," Jack said. He looked around to see if any of his fellow officers were in earshot. "It's a thing, a spirit…Banister called it a demon. It killed Banister to send me a message. We're in danger, Clem."

"Jack…" Clemmie interrupted with skepticism.

"I've seen it, Clem. It's what I shot at in the hall of your mother's apartment building. It spoke to me. It spoke to me through William when Banister drugged him. And it spoke to me as I stood next to the staircase. I shot it, Clem. I shot it twice. The bullets went right through it. How do you get rid of something that can't die?"

Clementine saw for the first time in their relationship that her partner was in a panic. She had never seen this with Jack before. He was always in control…always knew what to do. She felt obligated to get Jack out of this spiral.

"Jack! Look at me!" Clemmie said, grabbing his face. "You're Detective Jack Banks of the Ninth Precinct. You have a problem in front of you. How do you fix it? You always figure out how to fix it! Do your job, Detective!"

Jack looked at his wife and nodded his head with gratitude. In his calmness, he vowed to protect his wife and defeat this "Gray." He just needed to be reminded of who he was and what the stakes were.

"You're always right, Clem. I fell into this...thing's trap. It craves fear. It wants to create it. It feeds on it," the detective explained. He cupped Clementine's face in his hand and told her, "We can't be afraid, Clem. We can't give in to fear."

"What have you told me countless times?" Clem asked. "Knowledge is power. You can't defeat anything without knowing your enemy."

"Yep. The last thing Banister told me was to find a priest," Jack muttered and then sighed. "It's going to take one hell of a special priest..."

"So, let's go find your priest," Clemmie told Jack determinately.

Jack did a take at his wife and said, "What do you mean 'let's?' This is not a committee thing, Clem. You need to stay out of it and stay here."

"But you said we're not safe anywhere," Clemmie argued. "There's safety in numbers."

"What about your mother?" Jack said, pointing down the hall at the office that had become their temporary home.

"Did this thing say anything about her?" she asked.

"Not exactly…," Jack mumbled.

"Well, there you go. She'll be fine. Me and you will look out for each other," Clemmie said while rubbing her husband's chest.

Jack knew how stubborn Clementine could be. Her determination was an attractive quality. However, her headstrong ways would sometimes get her into trouble. Although Jack thought it was a bad idea, he relented to his wife, for now, by nodding his head.

"So, Detective, where do we start?" asked Clemmie.

Jack sighed and thought for a minute. "Well, Chief Dooley's Irish Catholic. Let's go see if he knows a good man of the cloth."

*

The door to Chief Dooley's office was open. But Jack knocked anyway out of respect. Then he and Clementine entered without the chief's invitation.

"Got a minute, Chief?" asked Jack, sitting down in front of the chief's desk.

Dooley looked up from the paperwork on his desk and answered, "Do I have a choice?"

"We'll only take a minute," Jack replied. "I have a quick question."

Dooley sighed in frustration and said, "OK. Let's have it."

Jack rubbed his jaw and mouth. He was trying to figure out how to broach the subject without exposing too much of what was going on with Gray. He felt it was wrong to keep his chief in the dark. However, with the threats the spirit was issuing, the fewer people drawn in to what was happening, the better.

"Chief, I'm not a religious man. And I've been in the camp where I thought religion was mostly a bunch of mumbo jumbo. But now, with William, I think there's more mystery out there than I thought. You're a Catholic, Chief. I need a priest for him."

"A priest? Why? Is William dying?"

"Kinda…" Jack uttered.

"Kinda? How can somebody be 'kinda' dying?" Dooley asked. He was growing more frustrated with Jack's "case." He sighed and moved his readers to the top of his head. Looking directly at Jack, he said, "Detective, I've bent over backward to let you pursue this case with not a lot to show for it. Unless your man can provide some concrete evidence on these murders, he's out the door, to his place or sanitarium, I don't care which!"

Jack took a beat to let his boss calm himself before speaking. "We, both of us, appreciate what you've done, Chief. And right now, no one in this world can understand how much I wish I'd never met William. But he's the key to finding and putting away this killer. I know it."

"What makes that true?" asked Dooley.

Jack needed a good lie to keep his ruse going. "William's…special, Chief. I don't know if he's crazy or gifted. But he sees murders as they happen. He can describe them down to the type of knife that was used. And he's never been to the scene."

"But why the priest?" asked Dooley. "You're not telling me something, Banks. It's not smart to hide information from your superior."

Jack threw up his hands defensively. "I'm trying my best to get him to tell me everything. I tried a psychiatrist. He didn't get very far, even with drugs. I was hoping William might confess to a priest what he knows."

"How many straws are you gonna grab at before you realize this guy's a kook?" asked Dooley.

Clementine saw that her husband was at a stalemate with the chief. She felt it was time to intervene.

"Chief Dooley, may I speak?" she asked.

Exasperated, the chief rubbed his forehead. This pushed his readers further on top of his head. "Yes, Mrs. Banks?"

"When I first sat in this office, you bragged to me about how good Jack was at his job," she began.

Dooley cut his eyes back at Jack, "I don't remember saying that."

"Well, I do," said Clemmie. "I don't know about policework. However, I do know that Jack has been involved with a lot of murders lately. And all of them lead back to this man. I'm not begging, I'm asking. Let Jack follow this lead some more. All he's asking for is the name of a priest. Hopefully, it will help solve the cases, and you will get your detective back. And, more importantly, I get my husband and life back."

Dooley leaned back in his chair and folded his arms across his chest. "Well, I'll be damned. I've been 'Good Cop and Bad Copped.' You brought her along to sway me, didn't you, Jack?"

Jack shook his head and answered, "Hey, she forced her way in to come with me. I have no control over her."

Dooley scratched his head with both hands. He grabbed his readers and tossed them on his desk.

"I knew it was a bad idea to let her stay here. I'm sending you to Father Duncan. He does the last rites of the prisoners who die here."

As the chief wrote down the priest's address, Jack asked. "He's not your priest?"

Dooley looked up from writing, chuckled a little, and handed the address to Jack. "You think I'm going to send you to my parish with a cocka-mamey story? I'd be excommunicated. Now, get out of my office, the both of you!"

Jack grabbed the address and led Clemmie out of the office. "Thanks, Chief!"

Once out of Dooley's office, Clementine turned to Jack and smiled. She mouthed the word "teamwork" to him as they walked out of the precinct house.

*

The Church of the Blessed Sacrament was one of the older ones in the precinct. As Jack and Clemmie walked down the center aisle of the building's nave, they saw that it was empty. This wasn't a surprise, as it was a weekday afternoon and not a day of worship.

146

As they made their way toward the altar, a priest appeared from a side room. He was carrying several papers bound together with strings.

Jack quickened his pace towards the priest and called out, "Pardon me, Father, I'm Detective Jack Banks of the Ninth Precinct, and this is my wife, Clementine."

The priest continued toward the altar to unload his stacks of papers. As he walked, he asked, "Detective? Is someone dying in the jail?"

"Well, not yet," Jack answered. "I was sent here by Chief Dooley. We're looking for a…Father Duncan…"

"You're looking at him, my child," the priest said as he laid the papers on the podium. "How can I help you?"

"Well, it's a long ask," Jack began. He and Clemmie stopped at the base of the towering wooden altar and watched the priest descend from it to stand before them.

Duncan raised his open palms above his waist with an inviting gesture. He told them, "I'm here to help. What is the problem?"

"I need to talk to a priest who knows something about…" Jack hesitated for a second. Now that he was here, talking to a priest, he suddenly felt ridiculous. He thought that there was no way a rational man like himself would ever be talking to a priest about evil spirits. He cleared his throat and continued, "About demons."

Father Duncan's eyes grew wide with surprise. "Did I hear you correctly? You said, demons?"

"Listen, Father, I know it sounds far-fetched. But I have a man in a straitjacket in a jail cell that has, what I believe, a demon inside of him. And that demon can leave this man's body and kill people. It hacks them to pieces and feeds on their fear."

Father Duncan noticed an elderly couple enter the church. Another priest met them and was escorting them toward the confessional.

Duncan put his finger to his lips to stop Jack from talking. "Perhaps we should discuss this in a more private area. Come, the rectory is this way."

*

Father Duncan's rectory was in the basement of the church. With no windows, the lamps on his desk provided the only light. They cast a yellow light upon the priest, Jack, and Clemmie.

Jack had made his case to the priest, outlining all the traits William Arbogast was exhibiting. The projection of being somewhere else, feeling like he was committing the murders, and the other personalities that come through with different voices. Jack left nothing out, including describing the murder scenes in graphic detail.

"My God, Jack," Clemmie said in shock after learning everything her husband and William had been through. "Oh. Sorry, Father…"

"It's all right, my child. That was certainly a tale that earned a 'My God,'" Father Duncan said, leaning forward in his desk chair.

"So, what do you think, Father? Do you know somebody who can help me? Help William?" asked Jack.

"Well, dealing with demons is certainly not my forte," the priest began. "It's not like I could go down there and wave my hand over him and make this William fellow better. You're talking about wanting an exorcism. Something that I've never done."

"An exorcism?" asked Clemmie.

"It's a ritual…a ceremony to drive out the demon from a person's body," Duncan explained.

"Again, Father, do you know anybody who can perform one of those exorcisms?" Jack was becoming frustrated at the lack of progress. "It's kind of important. I'm trying to prevent more people from being hacked to pieces."

"You don't understand. Before any exorcism can be performed, an investigation must be conducted. And if enough evidence is found, the archbishop must finally approve it."

Jack folded his arms and said, "That seems like a long time."

Duncan smiled at the detective and said, "If there's one thing that the church likes, it's bureaucracy." The priest paused for a minute to think and then said, "There is one priest that I know around here who might help. Tell you what, I'll contact Father Garvey and we'll be at the precinct in the morning to visit with your William."

"How's eight in the morning?" asked Jack.

"Eight will be fine," answered the priest.

*

As they left the church, Clementine asked Jack, "You think the Father will help get rid of whatever this thing is?"

"I can only hope," answered Jack. "I'm betting Banister knew what he was talking about when he told me to get a priest."

As they passed a hotel on their way back to the precinct, Clementine grabbed Jack's arm to stop him. "Hey, do we have to sleep in the office again tonight?" she asked.

Jack noticed she had stopped him in front of the hotel. He smiled, cocked his head, and said, "What are you thinking, Mrs. Banks?"

"I'm thinking you could use a break from William and that…thing," said Clemmie. "How's about we get a room for the night and get… reacquainted? We can be back at the precinct in plenty of time to meet Father Duncan in the morning. Maybe this hotel will be a place where your thing can't find us?"

Jack thought for a minute of his responsibilities to his chief and William. But missing his wife's embrace overwhelmed his tired body and mind. He needed her. Jack looked into her entreating eyes and took her hands in his, smiling at Clemmie.

"I knew this teamwork concept was a bad idea," Jack said haltingly. "But you talked me into it, Mrs. Banks."

The Alibi

*

"How long are you gonna keep giving the guy shots, Doc?" the jailer asked Dr. Gordon. "I mean, he has to eat sometime…"

As Dr. Gordon knelt beside William's bed, he answered, "It is my sincere hope that this man is gone from here, soon, Tommy. Both the chief and I agree that he needs to be gone, hopefully, the next day or so. So, I will continue to follow Detective Banks's request to keep him sedated until the time comes to get rid of him."

Tommy smirked and said sarcastically, "Kind of a rotten bedside manner, Doc."

Gordon rose from his kneeling position and faced the jailer. "I don't care, Tommy."

The doctor left William's cell and climbed the stairs to the infirmary. He shut the door and locked it behind him. Sitting down at his desk, he pulled open a drawer to retrieve a fifth of whiskey. He popped the cork with his mouth and swallowed what could be counted as "more than a couple of shots."

His disdain for William did not rise from the pathetic man himself. He projected his hatred onto him for the disrespect he had endured at the hands of Dr. Banister during his treatment. It wasn't enough to suffer the daily indignity of treating petty thieves and miscreants. His opinion had been dismissed outright by someone who wasn't even familiar with the patient's situation. He was tired of the dismissals. He was tired of his position. He decided to finish the bottle before going home.

The whiskey had its own thoughts about Dr. Gordon leaving the infirmary. Gordon had shut his eyes and opened them to find it was midnight. He tried to rise from his desk chair and paused mid-rise, only to fall back into it. The doctor decided then and there that the chair was his bed for the night. He reached over the desk to turn off the lamp and closed his eyes to return to sleep.

Then, in the dark of the office, Dr. Gordon heard his office doorknob turn. He opened his eyes to see a dark silhouette standing in the doorway.

"Good evening, Doctor," said the voice of William.

"Arbogast?" asked Gordon in his drunken state. He had to squint to focus on the silhouette. "What are you doing here? How did you get out of your cell?"

The figure stepped into the room toward the doctor. The moonlight was just bright enough to bring a glint from the metal in the figure's hands. That's when Gordon realized the figure was holding a scalpel and a bone saw as he rushed towards him.

CHAPTER 13

The following morning was a blissful change for Jack and Clemmie. They woke up in each other's arms in the hotel room where they had hidden from their troubles. The night before was passionate, where the couple expressed how much they had missed each other. It led to the first good night's sleep either of them had experienced in days.

Jack was the first to awaken that morning. When he opened his eyes, he looked over at his wife and smiled. He relished the fact that his mate kept him sane and wanted to help him through this ordeal. He loved her more for it.

Not wanting to wake her and make her move, Jack slowly reached over to the bedside table and looked at his watch. It was 6:45 in the morning. He knew he had an appointment with the priests at eight o'clock. It was time to wake up Clemmie.

"Clem, Honey. It's time to get up," Jack said as he slid out from under Clementine.

Clemmie answered with a moan as her head fell to the pillow under her. "Is it morning already? What happened?"

"We happened, Clem. I think we were both tuckered out when we fell asleep," said Jack.

"Five more minutes?" she pleaded with her head buried in the pillow.

"Hey, Clem," he began. "We have the room till noon. You can stay here and check out then. I'll go and meet the priests."

Clemmie shook her head without raising it from the pillow. Lifting her arm, she spoke into it in a muffled, "Teamwork!"

Jack smacked his wife's butt cheek and said, "Then come on, we can't be late."

"Yes, Detective…" she groaned as she pushed her body up from the mattress and rolled onto her back.

*

The Banks had hurriedly dressed and made their way down the street to the precinct house. By Jack's estimation, they would beat the priests to the jail by 15 minutes.

They went through the door of the building, smiling at each other. But the smiles soon faded when they saw the pandemonium inside so early in the morning. Officers were scurrying about, some on the phone, while others expressed disgust at what they had seen upon arriving at work that morning.

"I've never seen such a mess!" said one officer.

"How come nobody heard what was going on?" asked another.

"Who's going to tell the wife?" asked a third.

"I'm not cleaning that up!" declared another.

Jack and Clementine looked upon the scene with utter confusion. Something had happened inside the jail, and they were trying to figure out what. It was all coming to them in waves.

"Banks! Get in here!" Chief Dooley screamed at his office door.

Jack and Clementine hurriedly complied. They rushed across the chaotic scene and entered the chief's office.

"What the hell, Chief?" Jack asked.

"Sit down!" Dooley commanded. Jack and Clemmie obeyed. "Where have you been? I've been trying to get hold of you since five this morning." "We decided to book a room at the hotel down the street," explained Clemmie. "We wanted to..."

"I'm not asking you, Mrs. Banks," Dooley interrupted. "I'm asking my subordinate. The one I can fire."

No one had to tell Jack he was in trouble with Dooley. For what, he hadn't figured out yet. The first thing was to explain why he was out of touch. He began, "Chief, we decided to hide out in a hotel room. It beats the hell out of sleeping on that office desk. Besides, we haven't been alone in a good while…"

"It was my idea," Clemmie said defensively.

"OK. We're guilty of a man and a wife wanting each other," Jack confessed. "Now, what is all the commotion about?"

"What it's about is Doctor Gordon. He was killed in the infirmary sometime this morning. Cut up just like your other victims. And the kicker is your little friend says he did it."

Shocked at the news, Jack could only ask, "William's awake?"

"Yes, William's awake," Dooley answered sarcastically. "He's awake because Gordon couldn't give him a shot."

"Is Gordon still in the infirmary?" Jack asked.

"He's all over the infirmary," Dooley answered.

Jack jumped up and ran out the door towards the stairs that led to Dr. Gordon's office. Clemmie followed him up the stairs. Jack stopped at the door and grabbed Clementine.

"What are you doing, Jack?" Clemmie said, trying to wrestle her arm from her husband's grip.

"I don't think you want to go in there, Clem," Jack said. "I've seen a few of these murders, and they're pretty gruesome."

"Jack, please," she protested. "I'm a nurse!"

Clementine jerked her arm away from Jack. She preceded her husband into Dr. Gordon's office.

What the couple witnessed was the complete obliteration of Dr. Gordon's body. The lower limbs had been severed and stacked behind the body's torso. Gordon's upper body was leaning against the severed limbs, and the ribcage had been broken apart at the sternum and spread open like a pair of butterfly wings. They were spread open to reveal the internal organs and Dr. Gordon's severed head, which had replaced the doctor's heart. The heart was lying on the blood-soaked floor along with the kidneys, liver, and other organs that had been removed from the chest cavity to make room for Gordon's head.

Clementine suppressed a scream with her hand over her mouth. She had anticipated blood, but not this level of gore and mutilation. She took a deep breath and said, "Oh my God, Jack! Have they all been like this?"

Jack shook his head and said, "No. The others' bodies were scattered about the rooms, except for the hands. This looks ceremonial. Scientific?"

"Like a dissection. An autopsy..." Clemmie said.

Jack stepped in front of Clementine and walked towards Dr. Gordon's corpse. He squatted down to look into the doctor's eyes, still wide with horror.

"Sorry, Doc," Jack said. "This is all my fault. If I had..."

The detective stopped himself when he saw the slip of paper that had been inserted into the doctor's mouth. He stood up and pulled out the paper. It had been torn off Gordon's prescription pad. The writing on it, again, was in blood. It had been folded in two. The outside read:

TO JACK BANKS

Jack opened the folded paper to read what was inside:

I DISPLAYED THE DOCTOR IN A MANNER BEFITTING HIS CALLING. CLEMMIE'S WILL BE JUST AS INTERESTING!

FREE WILLIAM!

This threat enraged Jack. He crumpled the paper into a wad and threw it onto the floor.

"What did it say, Jack?" asked Clementine.

Jack tried to calm himself before answering her. He leaned on the desk with his hand and took in a deep breath. "It said Doc Gordon was left like this because of his medical background," he explained. Jack turned around and headed toward Clementine and the office door. "C'mon, the priests should be here any minute. And if William's awake, I should talk to him."

"I really should check on Mother," Clemmie mumbled as he passed her. Still staring in horror at the corpse, she added, "I'll join you in a minute."

Clementine waited to hear Jack descending the stairs. She walked over to the crumbled-up wad of paper on the floor. Clemmie picked it up, stretched it out, and read it. After reading Gray's threat, she nodded and looked toward the door.

Clemmie realized Jack was protecting her. But it still made her mad that he was keeping things from her. She stuffed the note in her pocket and gazed at the poor doctor. It made her more determined to stop this thing.

*

William's jail cell door was open, with the jailer standing in it as a guard. Jack saw William sitting on his bed, still in a straitjacket. He was slowly rocking back and forth with his eyes closed.

"You can take a break, Tommy," said Jack, putting his hand on his shoulder. "I'll stay with him till my guests arrive."

"Guests?" Tommy asked. "I hope they have a longer life than your last 'guest!'"

Jack smiled sarcastically. "You're hilarious! Now, get lost."

The detective sat next to the rocking William and began, "William, I…"

William snapped his head around to look at Jack. The look in his eyes revealed a mix of panic and hopelessness.

"Put me back to sleep, Detective! Or kill me! I can't exist like this anymore. I didn't want to kill the doctor. I can't kill again!"

Jack grabbed William's face to keep his attention, "You know better, William. It's that thing with you. He wants you to see it kill. He's feeding on your fear!"

"Then, end me!" William screamed. He followed the plea with a mournful bellow.

"Banks!" yelled Chief Dooley over William's moaning. "The priests are here!"

Jack rose from the bed and said, "Thanks, Chief, just in time."

Seeing the priests in the hall of the jail cells, Dooley waved to them to come to William's cell. Father Duncan was the first to come in. He was followed by a much younger priest, Father Garvey.

Father Duncan walked up to Dooley and laid his hand on the Chief's shoulder. Dooley reciprocated the gesture.

"Father, good of you to come on such short notice," Dooley said.

"Think nothing of it, Chief. I'm just glad I'm here and there's no death around," answered Duncan.

Jack was ready to speak up and tell the father about Dr. Gordon upstairs. He began, "Actually, Father…"

Dooley stopped Jack by shaking his head and said, "Not now, Banks!"

The detective relented and approached the two priests. He held out his hand to shake the young priest's hand. "I'm Detective Banks, and you are…?"

Father Duncan interrupted Jack and said, "My apologies. Where are my manners? This is Father Garvey. I spoke of him yesterday. He's here to do an investigation for the church. Perhaps he can help you with your case."

"'The case' is right over here!" William said from the corner of his bed in an unfamiliar voice. "Get those bastards out of here. They're not worthy to deal with me!"

Everyone turned to face William. Father Garvey finally spoke. He turned to Jack and said, "Nice to meet you, Detective. I guess I'm on the clock."

"Father, this is William Arbogast. He's an accountant by trade. He came in saying he had committed murders. Gory dissections of women and men. The problem is, I can prove he wasn't at the murder scene on at least a couple of occasions. I think he has a demon on him."

"A demon?" Father Garvey began. "That's a big assumption. Are you sure he's not just mentally disturbed? Has a mental expert examined him?"

"Yes, he was examined by an alienist, a psychiatrist," Jack affirmed.

"And what were his findings?" asked Garvey.

Jack sighed deeply and scratched the back of his head. He haltingly began, "He was murdered, Father, just like the rest of the victims. There was a note left for me by the murderer. It said he had absorbed the doctor…" Jack stopped and wondered if he should continue. "Now I'm going to sound crazy. But I talked to Dr. Banister after he died…through William, there. He said the killer was a demon."

Father Garvey nodded. "Interesting. There have been cases of multiple possessions…"

"It's more like they're being held inside William, Father, like prisoners. I think this thing feeds off their fear," Jack said.

Garvey nodded again. He turned toward William and knelt in front of him. He took William's head in his hands and began examining him. William struggled and shook his head, trying to free himself of the priest's hands.

Clementine entered the cell behind the priests. As she stood beside Jack, she reached into her pocket and pulled out the note. She handed it to Jack.

"You forgot this," was all she said.

Jack's shoulders dropped in shame. Not wanting to interrupt the priests, he looked up to his wife and mouthed, "I'm sorry."

Clementine folded her arms across her chest. She shook her head at her husband.

"Leave me, priest! This is your only warning!" a voice out of William shouted. *"TE INTERFICIAM!"*

"What the hell was that?" asked Jack.

"It's Latin, Detective," Father Duncan explained. "He just threatened to kill him."

William's struggles began to contort his body. He was doing all he could while inside a straitjacket to get away from Father Garvey. The demon inside William exclaimed, *"AD INFEROS! ME SOLUM RELINQUATIS!"*

"Now what?" asked Chief Dooley.

"It just told us to leave him alone and...to go to hell," said Father Duncan.

"This is new," Jack said. "It's never spoken Latin to me.

162

"It's never had priests around that spoke Latin," Garvey said. He had to raise his voice over the moans of the twisting body of William.

Father Garvey released William and stood. He looked at Father Duncan as he reached into his coat pocket. He pulled out a small glass vial and showed it to Father Duncan. The elder priest nodded in approval.

Father Garvey uncorked the vial and proceeded to sprinkle its contents upon William's head. He continued until the vial was empty.

William screamed in pain. He began to writhe on the bed, trying his best to get into a position to rub the substance from his scalp.

"URIT!" it screamed. Then, William seemed to return to his body. "It burns! It burns!"

With compassion toward William, Jack spoke up, "Hey, I didn't bring you here to torture the poor guy. What's the idea of dumping acid on him?"

"Not acid, Detective," said Father Garvey. "It's holy water. I didn't want anyone to know in advance what my actions would be, in case Mr. Arbogast tried to fake his reaction. It was my final test. Only a demon would react that way to water blessed by a priest."

Father Duncan nodded. "I agree. We're dealing with something dangerous here."

Jack weighed in, "I think I said that."

"Indeed, you did, Detective," Duncan said. He turned to Dooley and added. "Chief, I think it would be best to take Mr. Arbogast and put him in a safer environment. Under our care, of course."

Dooley chuckled, "Suits me. I've been on Banks to get rid of the guy for days. You can have him."

William suddenly jumped up from the bed and shouted, *"Non Ibo!"* He started fighting and struggling with the straitjacket once more. Only this time, the seams holding the belt restraints started to tear away from the jacket. William's emaciated body was suddenly surging with the strength of several men. With his arms free, he tore off the straitjacket and lunged at the priests. The three men landed on the hard cell floor in a pile. With the new superior strength, William was more than a match for the two priests.

"Jailer! Tommy! Get down here!" Dooley yelled down the hall for assistance. Then he jumped onto the attacker's back. William's body was still winning the fight. He threw off the chief with one arm. Dooley quickly got up and jumped on him again.

"Clem! Get out of here!" Jack told Clementine. Then, he grabbed her by the arm to stop her. He pointed towards the infirmary and said, "No! Go to Gordon's office and get a sedative! Hurry!"

Clemmie nodded, and she was off. Jack then joined the fight to pull William off the priests and hold him.

When the jailer came through the cell door, he also joined the chief and Jack. The three, along with the priests, were finally successful in restraining him.

"Anybody got any cuffs?" asked Dooley.

"You think I'm gonna let go to find some?" Jack said, trying to control one of William's arms. "Clemmie! Hurry up!"

Clementine flew up the stairs to Dr. Gordon's infirmary. She went to the medicine cabinet and found it was locked, as it should be. She spun around the infirmary, looking for any open vials. Nothing. Hearing her husband's pleas for haste, she had to force herself to go back to Gordon's office. Taking a deep breath to calm herself, she slipped past the doctor's corpse to the back of the desk and began opening drawers.

In the middle drawer, she found the vial Gordon had been using to sedate William, along with a syringe.

She rushed back down the stairs to William's cell. She could hear William screaming, *"NON IBO!* I won't go!" all the way back. Clem found that additional officers had joined in, trying to hold William's body down.

Jack saw his wife at the cell door and yelled, "Let her in. She's got a shot!"

Two officers made room so Clementine could stand beside Jack. She filled the hypodermic with the sedative, stabbed William's neck, and administered the shot.

Soon, the struggling prisoner began to fade. His screams of *"NON IBO"* were reduced to mumbles. Then the eyes closed, and the gang restraining William's body picked him up and laid him on the bed.

"He's all yours, Father," a heaving and out-of-breath Chief Dooley told Duncan. "Pardon my French, but get this son of a bitch outta my jail!"

Kelly Key

CHAPTER 14

The 9th Precinct's paddy wagon pulled up to The Church of the Blessed Sacrament's front steps. The driver came around the back of the wagon to open the large double doors. They could not be opened from the inside of the box on the back of the wagon.

Jack was the first to jump down to the sidewalk. He turned back to the wagon to help Clementine down and then pulled on the handles of the stretcher, to which heavy leather straps had tightly restrained William Arbogast. His wrists and ankles were restrained, buckled to the larger straps that wrapped around the stretcher. Fathers Garvey and Duncan brought up the rear, each holding a side of the stretcher.

As the wagon pulled away, Jack and the priests carried the stretcher toward the front steps of the church. Just then, William began to stir and resist against his bonds. His eyes suddenly opened, and he let out a garbled scream.

Jack looked down at William to see if he was going to say anything. When the detective looked back up, there was the transparent image of William standing between the stretcher carriers and the church.

"Gray…" Jack said under his breath.

Both Father Duncan and Garvey gazed upon the visage in front of them. They looked down at William to confirm it was the same face. Then they looked back at each other.

"Let's put Mr. Arbogast down," said Father Duncan. The three men placed the stretcher on the sidewalk, and the two priests came around Jack to stand side by side in front of the demon.

"You have no authority here!" yelled Father Garvey. "Leave, demon!"

"You're wrong…Father," the demon said, calling out the title in a derogatory tone. It pointed at William on the stretcher and said, "I have control of that one. I want him back. He is my possession."

"He is under our care now," said Father Duncan. "He will not service you anymore. Now, be gone! The power of Christ compels you!"

Father Garvey retrieved another vial of holy water from his jacket. He bit off the cork and slung holy water at the ethereal likeness of William. The liquid splashed on the demon's face. But it was William, restrained on the stretcher, who cried out. Welts and blisters appeared on his face as if the water had splashed on him.

"It burns! It burns!" screamed William.

A look of indignation fell across the demon's face. And just as quickly as the demon had appeared, he was gone in a wisp of vapor.

Father Garvey took a step forward to stand where the demon had appeared. Deep in thought, the priest nodded his head and uttered, "Interesting…"

"Interesting?" yelled a disturbed Clemmie. "I'd say scary as hell!"

Jack put his arm around his wife to reassure her and commented, "You'll have to give me some of that water, Father. It works a hellava lot better than bullets in fighting that thing."

"You'll find that our arsenal of weapons has been proven over the centuries to defeat the evil ones," said Father Duncan. "No magic, no potions, or conventional weapons have more power than the power of Christ against them, Detective. It all comes down to faith."

Father Garvey turned to the others standing around the stretcher. "Come on. We need to get Mr. Arbogast inside the sanctuary. I have a room prepared for him."

They picked up the stretcher and carried it up the church's front steps. A semi-conscious William was still writhing from the pain of the burning waters.

*

William was placed in a chamber deep in the church's undercroft. There were no windows in the room, only a bed with a table beside it. A coal oil lamp and a Bible were the room's only other decorations. The lamplight threw long shadows on the stone walls.

William was placed on the bed. His leather restraints were transferred from the stretcher to the bed. His wrists and ankles were bound to the frame of the bed because the frame was made of metal. Garvey thought the new strength William had shown at the jail would break the wooden bedposts if the demon decided to resist again. Even with all the draconian ties, they tried to make the bed as comfortable as possible for William. He was a victim, after all.

Jack and Clementine waited outside the room for Father Garvey to emerge from it. The priest finally left William. He shut the door to the room as he came out.

"What now, Father?" Jack asked.

Father Garvey sighed and said, "Well, for now, we'll have to wait for the chemicals to leave his system."

"You think that's a good idea?" Jack asked. "I know for a fact that when William's not drugged, people die."

"William has to have his faculties to fight off the demon," Garvey explained. "We can't just chase it away. William must reject it of his own free will."

"All I know is it likes to see William scared," said Jack. "And that usually leads to somebody dead. It might be out there right now…"

"Perhaps, Detective, but unlikely. Did you see what I saw happen with the holy water?" Garvey asked.

"Yeah," said Jack. "The demon hurt William."

"No, the holy water hurt the demon and William because…"

"He was still inside of William!" Jack interrupted with his epiphany. "What we saw was only a vision! A projection! You could see through him. He wasn't solid like before."

"Very good, Detective," complimented Garvey. "We might make an exorcist out of you yet. The demon could only manifest a vision of itself. I believe it took all its strength to create that ghostly vision. Now, whether that was because of the drugs in William, we will have to see."

"And since the drugs were wearing off at the precinct house, that enabled the thing to form and kill Doc Gordon," said Jack.

"More than likely," answered Garvey. "It will be at full strength once the chemicals wear off."

"That sure is a big old fire you're playing with, Father," Clementine said. "I hope you know what you're doing…"

"Don't let this boyish face fool you, Mrs. Banks," the father said with a smile. "A little knowledge and a lot of faith go a long way in these cases."

"I think we'll need a wagon full!" Clem said emphatically.

Sensing Clementine's real fear, Father Garvey was empathetic towards her concerns. He turned to Jack and said, "Detective, now that Mr. Arbogast is in our care, there's really no need for you to be here. It's our struggle now. You and Mrs. Banks can go."

Jack looked up at the priest, his face filled with anger and determination. "Oh, no! We're here till that thing is gone! Clem, show Father Garvey that note you picked up in Doc Gordon's office."

Clementine reached into her dress pocket and retrieved the warning, written in the doctor's blood, addressed to her husband. She handed it to the priest.

While Father Garvey read the note, Jack said, "See, Father. This thing has made it personal…for me and Clementine. If we leave, he'll find us—especially if you wean William off the drugs. We're not going anywhere!"

Father Garvey nodded after reading the note. He handed it back to Clementine and said, "Perhaps you're right. Logically, this would be the safest place for your protection. I was only thinking of Mrs. Banks's mental welfare…"

"Please, no more 'Mrs. Banks.' Call me Clementine. And sometimes fear is the greatest defense. It makes you think of the best way out. Just because I'm afraid doesn't mean I'm ready to quit. My husband and I are a team on this case. Father, you just joined the team."

Father Garvey chuckled and said, "Well, then, my child…I mean…Clementine. Looks like we'll fight this thing together. That note of yours spoke of 'Freeing William.' That's just what we're going to do."

From behind the closed door came a scream, "Staying here won't save you! I'll kill you all and take this place down, too!"

A loud shriek followed the demon's statement and chilling laugh. Father Garvey told the Bankses, "Just to prepare you, the threats and howls are a large part of this. Just remember, it's not Arbogast. It's the demon. It is in a position to want to hurt us anyway it can—physically, verbally. It will stop at nothing to keep Arbogast."

"I know that now, Father," Jack said. "Makes me feel bad about all those times I let loose on William. It probably only made his fear worse."

"Don't beat yourself up, Detective. You're no longer ignorant of his situation," Garvey said.

"Okay, Father, what exactly is his 'situation'?" asked Clementine. "You keep saying it's a demon. What is it?"

"Well, from my observations and what Detective Banks…"

"Jack, Father," requested the detective.

"Yes, well, what Jack has told me is that this is more than a possession. This demon is like a parasite, a tick, if you will—feeding off of the fear of the possessed and the victims. This is connected to the condition of oppression, where the demon torments the victim with acts and misfortunes. Showing the murders as if the victim is doing it makes me think of the term *'dédoublement,'* a French term meaning being in two places at once. Mr. Arbogast has a very evil spirit attached to him."

"It calls itself 'Gray'," Jack added.

Garvey chuckled again, "How clever and random. Its main purpose is to deceive us, Jack. I'm sure it has gone by many names over the centuries. We may never know its real name."

"Well, I vote for 'Son of a Bitch'," said Clementine. She caught herself, realizing she was in a church and that a priest was present; she added, "Sorry, Father…"

"Swearing is appropriate in this case, Clementine. I'm sure after we start, you'll hear more than your share of foul language from the demon," said Garvey. "Now, while we wait, I have to confer with Father Duncan about how we proceed. There is always food in the kitchen if you're hungry."

"Thanks, Father," said Jack. "I could eat." Jack turned to his wife and asked, "Clem?"

"I'm not hungry," she answered. "But getting out of here for a while, I think, is a wonderful idea."

Jack wrapped his arm around Clemmie and said, "Come on."

As they turned to follow the priest down the hallway in the Undercroft of the church, the voice from behind the door howled and pleaded, "Clemmie! Clemmie! Don't leave me!"

Clementine froze in her tracks. "That sounded like Mother!"

Father Garvey placed a comforting hand on Clementine's shoulder. "This demon's a trickster. It will use other people's voices to instill fear and doubt in us. Besides, we've seen that it won't be able to manifest its body till the drugs release him. She should be alright."

"Yeah, well, it's been known to absorb souls, so it can still feed off them," said Jack. "I talked to Dr. Banister after he had been hacked up. You got a phone, Father? I think I'd better call into the station to check on Clem's mother…just in case."

"Yes, there's one in Father Duncan's office," Garvey said as he pointed down the hall. "This way."

"Clemmie! Clemmieeeeeeeee!" the demon wailed in Gladys's moaning voice.

Clementine shuddered and covered her ears to block the demon's calls. Father Garvey put his hand on her shoulder and led her down the dark corridor. He looked back at the closed door, dreading the duties to come.

*

"Ninth Precinct, Dooley speaking," the chief answered after taking the receiver off the switch hook of the candlestick phone on his desk.

"Chief? It's Clementine," she responded. Jack thought that her calling would lessen the chances of Chief Dooley yelling at him again. "Is my mother available to talk?"

"Hello, Clem," answered the chief. "I'll have somebody get her. Jackson! Go tell Mrs. Banks's mother that she has a phone call and bring her in here!" he yelled. "Sorry for being loud, Clem. It's still a circus here. Most of the men not on patrol are up in Dr. Gordon's infirmary, um, gathering evidence. That's why I'm answering the phone. Now, while we're waiting, can you tell me when your husband is coming back to work?"

"Um, that's a good question," said Clementine, stalling for time. She looked at her husband for help.

Jack nodded and relented. He took the phone from his wife.

"Hey, Chief," Jack said in a subdued tone.

"Banks? Did you deliver Arbogast to the church?" asked the chief.

"Yes, sir. We're here now," Jack answered.

"Well, you're done then. Get back here and find the real killer of Gordon!" Dooley demanded.

"I think he's here, Chief. Or, I should say, it's here," said Jack.

"Damnit, Jack! I'm tired of hearing all of this mystical mumbo jumbo! I'm beginning to believe you've taken leave of your senses!"

"You might be right, Chief..." Jack responded, thinking that agreeing with him might calm his superior. And, in a little way, Jack thought so, too.

"Don't agree with me to make me shut up, Jack. I need a detective who deals with facts, not faith. Banks, I'm this close to canning your ass! Hell, I'd fire you right now if Clem's mother wasn't here!" Dooley said as he waved Gladys to come in and sit in the chair in front of his desk.

"I'll try my best to explain everything to you, Chief. But Clem and I have one last thing to take care of before I'm finished. I hope you'll have patience enough to wait."

Chief Dooley waited a beat to seethe. Looking at Clementine's mother, he told Jack, "Get your ass in here in the morning or there'll be hell to pay!"

Handing the phone to Gladys, Chief Dooley added, "Pardon my French, miss. Your daughter wants to talk to you."

Gladys took the phone and held the receiver to her ear. Raising the carbon microphone to her face, she asked, "Clemmie?"

Jack blew out a relieved sigh and handed the phone back to Clementine. She smiled in anticipation and relief that her mother could talk to her.

"Mother? Are you OK?" asked Clementine.

"OK?" asked Gladys. "I'm away from home and sleeping on a cot in a cold office!"

Her complaining made Clementine smile. She knew as long as her mother was complaining, she was fine. "We hope to get you home soon, Mother."

"Soon sounds vague. When are you coming to get me?" Gladys asked.

"We have something to do here at the church. Just as soon as it's done, we'll all go home," explained Clementine.

"Well, make it quick. This place is giving me nightmares. Last night I dreamed a man was chasing me."

A look of horror fell over Clementine's face. "Mother…can you describe what he looked like?" she asked.

"I don't remember much, Clemmie," said Gladys. "It was just a dream. I'm glad it's over."

"Was he a small man with dark hair?" asked Clemmie.

"I think so. How did you know?" asked Gladys.

Jack turned to the priests sitting around the desk. He had the look of confirmation in his eyes that clearly said, "See!"

Clementine shut her eyes and paused. She was trying to think of how to explain something she could hardly believe herself. She finally went with, "You remember the man Jack shot at? I think this dream has something to do with him. Mother, listen. If you have that dream again, do all you can to stay away from him."

"I don't know what you're worried about. I won't dream it again," scoffed Gladys.

"Just please do it!" Clementine said frantically. "The man in your dream is a killer!"

"Now you're talking nonsense," Gladys said. She looked up at Chief Dooley and commented, "The things I put up with, Chief. You have no idea."

Dooley just shut his eyes and shook his head. "Madam, you are holding up the line on a police phone. You need to hang up, soon."

"Oh, now the police are telling me what to do," complained Gladys. "Clemmie, I have to go. The police need this line."

"Just be careful, Mother. We'll pick you up as soon as we can," said Clemmie. Without saying goodbye, she hung the receiver back on the phone's tower.

"That thing's not only after me and Jack! Now it's after my mother!" Clemmie exclaimed. She sat down on Father Duncan's desk and began to weep. She had finally been overwhelmed by the day's events. A feeling of inevitable dread and hopelessness washed over her.

Now it was Jack's turn to pull Clementine out of a dark spiral. He went over to her and placed his hands on her face.

"Hey, HEY! Look at me, Clem. Don't let the demon get you. We're in the right place with the right people to fight this thing. We're almost home, honey. Don't let him win!" Jack let go of her face and drew her into a firm embrace.

Resting her head on her husband's shoulder. "Dammit, Jack, what are we doing? We can't leave, and when that thing wakes up, he's liable to go after Mother!"

"We're working on that, Clementine," Father Garvey said from across the desk. "We have to have a plan before we start. Now, as I mentioned, I would like to confer with Father Duncan on how we proceed. Once we have a strategy in place, we can tell you the part you can play."

Father Duncan stood from his chair and walked over to the Bankses. "We have so little time, Mr. and Mrs. Banks...I mean, Jack and Clementine. Please allow us to map out a plan, and we'll meet afterward. Father Garvey told me you could use some food? The kitchen's just down the hall and to the right. The food is plain, but abundant."

Jack pulled away from Clementine and said, "You giving us the bum's rush, Father?"

"For lack of a better way to say it, yes," said Duncan.

"I do like an honest priest," Jack joked. "C'mon, Clem. Let's let them do their job. We'll be right down the hall."

"Thank you for understanding, Detective," said Duncan. He gestured with his right arm while leading them through the door. "Down the hall, to the right."

*

Father Duncan shut the door and turned to Father Garvey. "Father Garvey, I have concerns about Mrs. Banks."

"As do I," Garvey said, rising from the chair. "Clementine is a strong woman. But if our demon friend discovers she can be manipulated, he will use her. Feed on her fear."

"It's a factor we'll have to keep in our minds. We might have to save Arbogast…and her as well."

CHAPTER 15

Jack and Clementine found the church's kitchen to be sizeable and tidy. Several large pots were hanging from hooks in the ceiling above the counters. Huge gas stoves with multiple ovens lined the back wall next to the sinks. Seeing no food out, they had to search the cabinets for something to eat.

"This is a giant icebox!" Jack declared. "How many people are they feeding?"

"The church serves as a soup kitchen, honey," explained Clementine. "They must come in here mornings and prepare meals for the poor."

"That sounds like something the priests would do," said Jack. He opened the icebox door and asked her, "What are you hungry for? There's milk and cheese and ham…"

"I'm not hungry," answered Clementine. "How can you think of food with all this going on?"

"Clem, neither of us has eaten since yesterday. We gotta keep our strength up. You heard the priests. It's going to get rocky in the next few hours. We have to be strong," said Jack. He reached into the icebox, turned, and tossed an apple at her. Clementine caught it with both hands. "Come on, Clem, for me?"

Clementine shook her head and bit into the red apple. "Jack, what are we doing? You heard the Father. We can go. Let's get out of here."

"And go where, Clem?" asked Jack as he sliced at the large ham. "That thing somehow knows where we are at any time. He found our apartment, for God's sake. If we're going to have any peace in our lives, we have to make sure it won't bother us or anyone else again. I can't let it keep killing. I think the priests are our best bet."

"You said yourself it can't be killed, Jack," said Clementine. "What if it won't go?"

Jack stopped making his sandwich and thought a moment before saying, "I know it's a long shot. But I'm hoping William has enough left in him to banish that demon."

"And I'm hoping those words don't come back and bite you in the ass," said Clementine, taking another bite of the apple.

"William wants to do what's right. Now he has the right help," Jack said. He finished building his ham sandwich and took a large bite.

With a light rap on the kitchen doorway, Father Duncan entered the kitchen. "Pardon the interruption, my children. But we're getting ready to begin."

Jack swallowed a big chunk of his sandwich and said, "Great, Father. What do we need to do?"

"Father Garvey will lead the exorcism," Duncan said. "He'll begin with a prayer of protection. It's called The Prayer to Saint Michael the Archangel. Otherwise, you, being helpers as I am, follow my lead and don't hinder him. This isn't Father Garvey's first exorcism. He knows what he is doing. Now, if you'll come with me, we'll begin."

Both Jack and Clementine swallowed the food in their mouths hard. They looked to each other for solace and found the determination to follow Father Duncan out of the kitchen to meet up with the exorcist.

*

As the three entered Father Duncan's office, they found that Father Garvey had changed into a different set of raiment. Dressed in a white Alb (or tunic), the priest wore an embroidered white surplice over it. A purple stole was draped around his neck. Also hanging from his neck was a golden chain with a crucifix.

"Father Garvey, we're ready," declared Father Duncan.

"Very well," answered Garvey. "Please join me in prayer."

The four instinctively formed a small circle, and Father Garvey began the prayer.

"Saint Michael the Archangel, defend us in battle. Be our protection against the wickedness and snares of the devil. May God rebuke him, we humbly pray; and do thou, O Prince of the Heavenly Host, by the power of God, cast into hell Satan and all evil spirits who prowl about the world for the ruin of souls. Amen."

"Amen," said the others.

"Now, my children, as we go into that room, remember not to believe anything the demon says to you. It's a trickster," explained Father Garvey. "It wants to get out of this situation any way it can. It will say the most hurtful things it can think of. Ignore him and follow my lead."

*

The four left Duncan's office to make their way to the room where William was restrained. They began to hear William's voice coming through the door.

"Garvey! Duncan! Don't come in here! It will be your doom!" growled the voice. It was so loud that it reverberated up and down the hall in a continuous echo. Its volume increased as they neared the door.

"You have been warned! Stay out!" the voice added. It sounded more aggressive as they approached the room.

Garvey stopped before reaching the door. He turned to the other three and said, "Remember, if this demon does indeed feed on fear, we dare not show it. God is with us. Never forget that."

The priest pulled back the latch that had locked the door and opened it. When the four entered the room, they found William heaving with labored breathing. Duncan and Clementine rushed to the bed to gauge the bound man's condition.

"William? It's Father Duncan. Can you hear me?" he asked.

William opened his eyes and looked around the room. He squinted and saw Duncan and Clementine standing over him. "Where am I?"

"You're in a room below The Church of the Blessed Sacrament, my church. We're going to help you get rid of the demon possessing you."

"It's gone," said William.

"Gone?" asked a confused Garvey.

"It's taken off. I can't feel it or any other souls with me," William said.

"I told you, Father," said Jack. "As soon as William was conscious, that thing would take off."

"Mother..." mumbled a worried Clementine.

As their eyes were on William, the four didn't see the open door move away from the wall. But William did. He noticed the door slowly swing back to the doorway. There stood Gray.

"It's behind you!" William screamed.

Being behind the priests, Jack swung around to see a smiling doppelganger of William before him. Instinctively, the detective started swinging at the figure. He landed a solid punch on its jaw. He then threw another punch with his left hand, landing on the other side of its face.

Unflinching and unmoved, the thing grabbed hold of Jack's shirt and tossed him across the room. Jack hit the stone wall with his body and collapsed onto the floor.

"Jack!" screamed Clementine. She ran over to her husband to see if he was injured. By the time she reached him, Jack was helping himself up off the floor.

"I'm OK, Clem," he told her reassuringly. He struggled to catch his breath as it had been knocked out of him.

"You are not welcome in this house of God!" yelled Father Garvey at the demon. "In the name of the Father, the Son, and the Holy Spirit, I command you to leave!"

The priest then reached into his robe and pulled out a large bottle of holy water. He released the cork and splashed the thing's face. As the water ran down the face, it began to sizzle and hiss, burning its way into the flesh.

Father Duncan instantly turned to look at William. This time, he was unharmed.

The demon raised his head and smiled. He wiped the steaming holy water off his face with his sleeve. The scars from the burning water faded and healed. And in an instant, the demon was gone. It had disappeared before them. The open door suddenly slammed shut with a thundering bang, as if the thing had closed it.

"Are you alright, Detective?" asked Father Duncan.

Jack chuckled and replied, "For a guy that was just thrown into a stone wall at a hundred miles an hour, just peachy!"

"What were you thinking, Jack?" chided Clementine. "We've seen what it can do to people."

"Seemed like the best thing to do at the time," Jack replied. "Besides, it felt good to get a few licks in on that monster. I've been wanting to do that for a long time."

"Father Garvey, come look at this," Duncan said.

The exorcist came to Father Duncan's side. Duncan had William's face in his hand. He slowly turned it from side to side. Although William's face was ashen and sweaty, it was not harmed by Garvey's attack on the demon.

"We all saw the holy water sear into the thing's flesh," Duncan said. "But William's remained unharmed."

Father Garvey took the lamp from the bedside table and held it close to William's face. "Interesting. Since William is back and no longer feels its presence, we have to assume it has gone to feed and regain its strength."

"By 'feed' you mean kill!" Clementine said. "What if it's gone after Mother?"

"We don't know that, Clem," said Jack, trying to calm her.

"Well, I'm going to find out! Father, I need to borrow your phone again!" said a panicked Clementine as she ran across the room to the door.

"It would be best if we stuck together!" Duncan protested.

Clementine reached the door. She twisted the knob and pulled. Nothing happened. She pulled again, and the door would not open.

"It's locked!" she screamed. "That son of a bitch locked us in!"

Jack went over to the door and tried to open it. It wouldn't budge. He pulled again with the same luck. Finally, he banged on the door with his hand in frustration.

The two priests exchanged a glance. Then Duncan said, "Please calm yourselves. This is one of the many tricks it's using to make us panic—to instill fear into our hearts. We're here to defeat evil. We cannot defeat anything from the side of fear."

"Well, it looks like we're in here till the end, Father," said Jack. "What if it doesn't come back?"

"It will return, Jack," said Garvey. "It wants William too much."

Garvey turned back to William. Standing over him, he asked, "William, you see its murders. Can you see it now?"

William closed his eyes to see. "It's not showing me anything…Wait! The altar! A boy! Jesus!"

∗

Jimmy Marone had been an altar boy for over a year. One of the many tasks assigned to him was to extinguish the rows of burning candles after mass. Using the crooked candle lighter, he placed the snuffer bell at the end of the hook to "snuff out" the candle flame. There was a bank of burning candles before him at the altar. This was a tedious chore. However, there were worse ones to be done around the church. Jimmy liked to take his time with the candles and put off those chores.

"Excuse me, son," said a man who had come up behind Jimmy.

Jimmy finished the candle in front of him before turning to the voice, "Yes, sir. Can I help you?"

"I'm a bit lost, um, what is your name?" he asked.

"My name's Jimmy," he replied.

"Jimmy!" he said. He put out his hand for the altar boy to shake. "My name's William. Nice to meet you. I was wondering if you could direct me to Father Duncan's office. I have a message from Detective Banks to give to him."

"Father Duncan's office is under the chapel," Jimmy answered. Thinking this was a good way to delay his duties, he volunteered, "C'mon. I'll show you."

"Now, there's a good lad," said William with a smile. "Which way are we going?"

"This is the way," Jimmy turned and headed toward the door beside the pulpit.

As soon as Jimmy turned away from him, the demon produced a knife and plunged it into the boy's throat. The demon then pulled it across the front of Jimmy's throat, almost severing his head from his body.

Jimmy tried to scream in fear and in pain. But the only sound he could produce was gurgling from the gushing blood. He soon dropped his candle lighter to the chapel floor with a clang and went limp into his attacker's arms.

The demon picked up the lifeless boy and held him above his head. Jimmy's blood was raining on the demon and the wooden floor of the church. It turned and, with one heave, threw Jimmy's body into the candles. Scattering like bowling pins, the still-burning candles went everywhere. Some rolled under the tapestries that adorned the back wall of the altar and set them ablaze. The burning tapestries then set the wooden altar on fire. The whole platform soon burst into flames uncontrollably.

*

"I killed that boy…I killed that boy!" William screamed. He was so upset that he broke one of the leather restraints from the bed.

Father Garvey grabbed the strap and tried to fasten it back while William struggled under him. "William, William! Listen to me! It's the demon! The demon we all want gone. Can you summon it back inside you? It's the best way to control the demon."

William stopped struggling and jerked his head to look at the priest. "Why would I want to summon him? But, he'll be back. He needs me to be afraid for his feeding!"

He closed his eyes for a minute and continued, "He's set the church on fire! We're trapped and we'll all burn!"

"That's your fear talking, William!" said Father Garvey. "Don't let it control you!"

William opened his eyes again and whispered, "More boys! And priests are coming. They're trying to put out the fire!"

"Oh, Saint Michael, protect them!" Father Duncan pleaded. "They don't know there is a demon amongst them."

"And we can't warn them!" Jack said. He went over to the door and pulled with all his might to open it, to no avail.

*

The priests and altar boys had shed their robes and frocks and were trying their best to beat out or smother the flames with them. The fire was still winning. Buckets of sand were brought out from the wings of the chapel and tossed into the inferno.

The demon William stood in front of the pews, watching the vain attempts by the order to save their chapel. It walked up behind one of the boys and sliced his throat. It then picked up the still-alive boy and threw him into the flames.

Father Malloy watched in horror as the demon killed the boy. He rushed over to the demon and tried to take the knife from its hand. It grabbed the priest's arm and began twisting it. Malloy screamed in pain as the arm was wrenched from its socket. Soon, the twisted skin began to tear away from his shoulder. The demon William then took the knife and sliced through the shredded skin that kept the arm hanging. It raised the severed arm and threw it into the flames.

"Help me!" Malloy pleaded before collapsing to the floor into a pool of his own blood.

The remaining boys abandoned the fire and ran to surround the demon and the fallen Father Malloy. It killed them all and threw every one of them into the fire.

*

"They're all dead..." whispered William, in a catatonic state. He stared straight ahead and tried to process the horror he had just witnessed. "They're all burning in the flames!"

Father Duncan sank to his knees in anguish, "My flock! My children! Mother of God, why?"

Clementine bent down and put her arm around Father Duncan to comfort him. She kissed his forehead and brought the father into her chest for solace.

"If I could have warned them...Told them to fight the demon with the Holy Spirit, not the body," cried Duncan. "I have brought a monster to my House of God!"

Clementine hugged the priest tighter and said, "Had you been there, you might have been killed, too. Here, we still have a fighting chance."

"Yeah, we can't let the bastard win. Especially now!" declared Jack.

"The fire's getting worse!" said a desperate William. "It's coming. And so is he!"

"William," began a determined Father Garvey, "before he returns, say that you accept Christ as your savior and you'll confess and renounce all your sins in the name of God!"

William came out of his faraway stare as if he had been slapped back to consciousness. And he looked at the priest, and he began to cry. He uttered, "I cannot."

A confused look fell over Father Garvey's face. He cocked his head to one side and asked, "Is this William? Or the demon talking?"

CHAPTER 16

"We are all here…" said William's voice with a growl. The demon within the accountant made William's mouth smirk in defiance and confidence.

Father Garvey stood over William's body. He raised a cross to William's head and declared, "I command you to release this man and return to hell, demon!"

Gray laughed sarcastically at the priest's command. It answered, "You think I'm from Hell? I am an entity all to myself. I have walked this earth ever since it came into existence. I serve no one—not your devil, Satan, or anything else. People think I'm a ghost, a shape shifter, a shadow walker—all types of names they've called me over the centuries. I am all they described and more. Your religion and faith cannot affect or influence me."

Father Garvey fumed with rage. He was determined to prove that what the demon was saying was a falsehood to manipulate them. The priest took the crucifix he was holding and pressed it against William's chest. Smoke began to rise from the flesh as the metal cross burned into the skin.

"No more lying, devil! Be gone!" shouted Father Garvey.

The demon inside William screamed in pain. As Garvey lifted the crucifix from William's chest, he saw it had seared a black cross into the skin.

William appeared to lose consciousness for a second. He then slowly opened his eyes and looked at Father Garvey. This time, it was William who spoke. He pleaded mournfully, "Kill me! Let me die!"

"You don't have to die, William! Let me help you. Renounce this demon and confess your sins. Accept Jesus Christ as your savior!"

"I can't, Father! Let me die!" cried William.

"Why can't you? The Lord will forgive your sins!" declared Garvey.

William's eyes closed and reopened with a squinting glare. "Oh, poor William won't tell you his little secret..." mocked the demon with a false pout.

"What secret?" asked a frustrated Jack. He thought he'd been around William enough to gain his trust on every subject.

"Oh, it's not my place," it said coyly. "I'm certainly not going to help this little weakling to confess his sins. He'll have to do it himself...but he won't."

Jack came forward to stand beside Father Garvey. He had pledged to help William. He felt that the man strapped down on the bed trusted him enough that the detective would be able to draw it out of him.

"William, can you hear me?" Jack asked as he kneeled beside the bed.

"Y-yes," whispered William, pitifully.

"C'mon, Arbogast, we're risking our lives so you can escape this thing. We're all going to be dead if you don't help us help you!" Jack declared. "The fire's getting closer, and we can't get out till that thing is gone!"

Father Garvey nodded with approval at Jack's approach. He leaned over the bed and said to William, "It's up to you, my child. Confess your sins so we can shed this demon together."

"What is it, William?" Jack asked. "What's so terrible that you can't tell us?"

Gray returned and declared, "Little William's in denial. He won't confess it because then it will become real to him."

"Is this true, William?" Jack asked. "What's this all about?"

"I can't...I didn't..." whispered Arbogast.'

"Ask him about his wife," said the demon.

"His wife?" asked Clementine.

"Rose..." moaned William.

Jack had never heard William say his wife's name before. "What about Rose, William?"

"She died," William said. "I watched her die."

Jack was frustrated. He said, "You told me she died. And your son?"

"That's right. Ask him about his unborn son," encouraged the demon enthusiastically.

"Harry…" William moaned.

"What happened to them, William?" Jack asked.

"I…can't. I didn't… I couldn't!" cried William. He broke down in sobs as he was overwhelmed in grief again.

"Is it about their deaths?" Jack surmised out loud.

"Very good, Detective," the demon said. "You should feel the fear that William has right now. It's delicious, making me stronger and stronger. I told you I wasn't going to help him confess his sins. But I can lead you to them…"

"What do you mean, demon? More lies?" asked Father Garvey as he reached into his pocket and placed his fingers around another bottle of holy water.

"I'm cut to the quick, Father," mocked the demon. "If you won't believe me, let me bring forth a man who was there."

"What are you talking about?" asked Jack.

"Remember Mallory Fullerton? William's partner and best friend? He's still in here. I stifled him. But he needs to tell you his story."

William's eyes shut, and another voice emerged from his lips, "Help me! Free me!"

"Mallory?" asked Jack.

"Another trick, Gray?" asked Father Duncan.

"I think it's Mallory Fullerton," said Jack. "I've talked with him before."

"I wasn't supposed to die," Fullerton began. "The beast was happy and content to keep feeding on my fear and rage for years to come. The demon was the one who lusted after Rose. It looked upon William as a milksop of a man, not deserving a woman like her. It drove me to flirt with her behind William's back. It used my body to seduce her. It felt the pleasure of the affair, and I bore the guilt of making William a cuckold. I didn't want to betray my friend. The thing inside me did the evil deed, not me."

"Oh my God!" said Clementine.

"The baby was the demon's!" realized Jack. "It made Fullerton make a demon spawn!"

Gray's voice returned in self-satisfaction, "We do what we must to get our way!" It followed that statement with a husky and hardy laugh.

"We're fortunate it died," commented Garvey.

"I lived long enough to impregnate Rose," Fullerton began again. "Then I was killed unexpectedly. As I lay dying, I felt the demon leave my body. But it pulled my soul out and took it. It wasn't finished feeding on my essence. It lept from me to William that day. So, I was a witness to Rose and William's fight."

"Fight?" asked Jack.

"Rose was under the demon's spell. Part of the seduction was her developing feelings towards me. She was distraught when she learned of my death. She tried to hide her grief from William. But he started to get suspicious. She was taking my death too hard in his eyes. He thought he should be the one grieving over his best friend's death, not her. He began to wonder how close she and I were."

Jack deduced where this was going. He was shocked at the implications. The William Arbogast that Jack had met was meek and mild. He seemed to be a man broken by his wife's death, not haunted by her murder. The detective stood up at the bedside of his bound suspect/victim in disbelief and bewilderment.

"William, did you kill your wife and her baby?" asked Jack.

William's voice came through and stated as he shook his head violently, "No! I didn't! I couldn't!"

"What happened during the fight, William?" asked Father Garvey.

"No! I won't tell!" declared the tormented man.

"C'mon, William!" Jack said sternly. "We're almost there. If you don't tell your side of the story, I'll get it from Fullerton!"

"Confess your sins, man!" commanded Father Duncan.

There was silence in the sealed room for several moments. All four of the team were waiting for William to make up his mind.

Suddenly, William's voice began to stammer. "I, I found a note. My suspicion was high, and I began to search through Rose's belongings. In her coat pocket in the closet was an envelope. It contained a love letter from Mallory, written a week before he was killed. He professed his love for Rose and invited her to *'leave that sorry excuse of a man and run away'* with him."

"What did you do, William?" Jack asked. "Tell us!"

William swallowed hard and continued in his own voice, "I had loved Rose with all my heart since the day we met. Then she and my best friend and partner stabbed that heart. I was incensed. I felt betrayed. I felt cuckolded and humiliated. It enraged me.

"I ran into the sitting room of the apartment, shoved the letter in Rose's face, and confronted her. She told me she'd never seen that note before. I told her I knew it was from Mallory because I recognized his handwriting. She broke down and confessed everything. But she wasn't sad, I found out. She was sad because he was dead. I could see that he had completely won her over, and she was actually proud to have found new love with him. Nothing could have hurt me more than losing her love. Then, she looked me in the eye and pronounced that the baby was Mallory's and she was glad it was. I struck her across the face with my open hand. My mind was whirling with all this new information. In that moment, I both loathed and loved my wife at the same time.

"The strike across the face shocked Rose. She told me she couldn't stand living with me any longer. She went and grabbed that same coat and headed toward the door. She was leaving me. I don't know why I ran after her. Pride? Not wanting the shame of an affair to get out? Owning my wife? The point is, I did go after her. I caught up to her at the edge of the stairs. I grabbed her by the shoulder and spun her around. She was furious that I followed her. She pushed herself away from me, and I grabbed her arms. The push and pull of our struggle caused her to retreat. As she reached the top of the stairs, one of her feet slipped on the stairs' landing, and she fell away from me. I watched her tumble and roll, screaming until she landed at the bottom in a pile. Her neck was broken, and the baby couldn't survive without her. I killed them both."

*

Above the room, the chapel fire had grown to an inferno. The rugs on the floor had acted as fuses, spreading the flames to the pews. As the aged wooden benches went up in flames, the fire was now too big for the local men to extinguish. The local fire department had been called. But they were at the other end of the borough. It would take precious minutes for the firemen to arrive.

Smoke had drifted down into the hallway and kitchen on the lower levels. It crept towards the door sealed by the demon.

Jack noticed the thin wisps of smoke rising from beneath the door. Father Duncan saw it, too. The smell of burning embers and putrid, burnt flesh from the killed boys and priests upstairs began to make itself known to the people in the room.

"Borrow your jacket, Father?" asked Jack.

"What?" asked Duncan. He then realized what the detective wanted with it. "Oh, yes, of course."

Jack took Father Duncan's coat and used it to fill the space between the bottom of the door and the stone floor. The smoke was thwarted from entering the room—for now.

"That should buy us some time," said Jack.

"You're only delaying the inevitable," stated Gray. "Dying by smoke is a much easier death than dying by flames. Just ask the poor altar boys upstairs. Perhaps they passed out from lack of blood before they felt the flames. One can only hope," it said sarcastically before laughing.

Clementine grabbed Jack's hand for comfort. He was comforted, too. He was beginning to believe that they might die. If the demon didn't kill them, the fire would. In a way, he was glad to be with his wife rather than to be separated from her.

This made him think about William's love for his wife. None of this would have happened if Gray hadn't wanted William to suffer so. Had William not found that note, he would possibly still be with Rose. It was the note that triggered the murder.

"Fullerton, did you write that note?" Jack shouted across the room.

"Fullerton is no longer available to you," growled Gray. "He has said enough."

"You wrote that note and put it in the coat pocket where William could find it," accused Jack.

"Perhaps, Detective," said the demon coyly. "William was taking too long to figure out what had happened. So, it was necessary to show him. But, since Mallory was with me, he did write it…in a roundabout way. William was already under my power. So, I made Mallory write it through him. I made William none the wiser that it was his hand used to write it."

201

"And it was you who tripped Rose, causing her to fall and die!" accused Jack.

"I wanted William to myself. His love for that woman was an impediment. But in my defense, if William hadn't chased after her, she would have survived...for a while," Gray explained.

"You killed your own child!" Clementine yelled.

"Yes. I did," Gray said matter-of-factly. "I can have children anytime. Let's call this one a 'casualty of war'..."

Suddenly, William spoke with renewed strength and outrage, "You son of a bitch! You Hell spawn! You killed my Rose just so you could feed off me?"

"Indeed, William," answered Gray. "Your fears are just the right kind for my tastes—apprehension, shame, and ignorance. You're the perfect food. I shall go on feeding on you forever!"

"Not if I can help it!" interrupted Father Garvey. Feeling William was ready to combat Gray, the priest opened his prayer book, gestured the sign of the cross with his right hand, and began:

"In the name of the Father, the Son, and the Holy Spirit...

"And I command all spirits associated with these unholy ties, links, and bondages to go immediately and directly to the foot of the cross. O Most Holy Spirit, enter into the empty spaces left by these spirits and fill William with your presence, love, and protection. Please do not allow these spirits to return."

The demon, Gray, screamed in protest. It was as if the very words were tormenting its soul. It made William wince and writhe against his bonds.

Unknown to the four standing near the bed, the demon had made progress against the straps. It felt the leather tearing as it applied its great strength and pressure against them. As they began to break, the demon tore them slowly, so as not to make a sound and alert Jack, Clementine, and the priests.

The tearing noises were muffled against the demon's screams and Garvey's yelling prayers in an attempt to be heard over them. The priest repeated the following prayer three times:

"In the Name of Jesus, I break all curses sent against you and all spells around you."

"In the Name of Jesus, I break all curses sent against you and all spells around you."

"In the Name of Jesus, I break all curses sent against you and all spells around you."

As Father Garvey continued, Clementine took it upon herself to monitor the fire's progress. She ran her hands down the wall facing the hallway. Then over the sealed door. Although not hot to the touch, there was a definite rise in temperature.

"It's getting warmer," she declared to the room. "The fire's coming!"

CHAPTER 17

"Yes, it's getting warmer!" teased the demon with menace. "The flames are coming. There is no escape. You will all die together!"

"Shut your mouth, Gray!" Jack screamed to be heard above the demon laughing and Father Garvey's chanting prayers.

"In the Name of Jesus, I break all curses sent against you and all spells around you.

"In the Name of Jesus, I break all curses sent against you and all spells around you.

"In the Name of Jesus, I break all curses sent against you and all spells around you."

"If you think your incantations and prayers will drive me away, you're a fool, priest!" mocked the demon with a growl.

Garvey continued, undisturbed by the taunts of the demon. He rocked back and forth, as if he were in a trance, as he read from his prayer book.

"I can feel your fear rising," it said. "Fear is my manna. I can never be satiated! How gracious of you all to make me stronger."

Just then, Father Duncan popped open a bottle of holy water and threw it in William's face. It caught the demon by surprise as it thought they were too worried about the coming fire to keep battling it. The body of William gasped in pain.

The demon in William glared at Duncan. Its eyes shrank to small slits as he nodded. "I'm going to kill you, Duncan, before the flames eat you alive."

"Saint Michael, preserve us!" Duncan yelled, determined to defeat this thing. He kneeled beside the bed and began to pray with Father Garvey.

With one last hard jerk, the demon inside of William tore the straps that imprisoned it to the bed. William's body rose straight up to stand on the mattress. The leather straps fell away from William's body like dead snakes. Gray tore off the last strap and threw it onto the floor. It looked down on Father Duncan and said, "I told you I'd kill you!"

Jack rushed across the room to defend the priest. When he reached the bed, the demon used William's body and swatted him away with one arm. Jack flew across the room, bounced off the wall, and landed in the far corner.

Father Garvey seemed unaware of what was going on. His eyes were shut, and he was deep in prayer. It took Jack crashing into the wall to rouse him from his trance. He then saw William's body standing over him and realized he was loose. He grabbed his cross out of his robes, stood up, and backed away from the bed, mumbling a prayer of salvation.

Duncan then seemed to be frozen in fear. He kept repeating, *"Saint Michael, Saint Michael…"*

The demon leaped from the bed and grabbed Father Duncan by the head. The priest struggled to free himself but was overpowered by the demon's strength. Instead of producing a knife or any weapon, it twisted the priest's head until his neck was broken, and his spine was severed.

Father Duncan went limp. His eyes betrayed the terror he was experiencing. He muttered something, but it wasn't loud enough to be understood.

Clementine screamed and ran over to Jack, still sitting on the floor, struggling to get his wind back from the collision with the wall.

The demon wasn't finished with the priest. Instead of being satisfied with his broken neck, it kept twisting his head, wringing the neck until it separated from Duncan's body. When the last skin and sinews tore apart, it smiled and held the bloody head of Father Duncan above its shoulders. Blood showered down onto the face of William from the torn neck of the priest. Gray then thrust it forward, as if it were a trophy. The thing inside of William shook it proudly in front of the remaining three. Gray began to laugh triumphantly.

"Leave us alone!" Clementine screamed, helping Jack to his feet. He immediately shoved Clementine back behind him and stood between her and the demon.

"You heard the lady!" Jack yelled. "William, are you in there? Can you hear me?"

Gray stopped laughing. Something changed about it. The body was now controlled by William, who stared at Father Duncan's head in panic, shame, and disgust. Although William had been made to watch many murders committed by the demon, he had never committed the murders with his own mortal hands. The demon was always outside, on its own. William realized that he was a real killer now. He screamed in agony and dropped Duncan's head. It rolled across the floor and stopped in front of Father Garvey.

"I killed a priest...I killed a priest!" William moaned. "It's turned me into a murderer!"

Jack nodded. "It was all this thing's evil till now, William. Look at the blood on your hands. The blood of a holy man! Reject this demon! Cast it out!"

"The thing's thousands of murders! My one murder!" William began. "They're all mortal sins. I'm just as bad as it is!"

"You can be saved, my child! You can be free of it!" Father Garvey had been brought back from his trance by the sight of his fellow priest's head at his feet.

"That's impossible now!" William yelled at the priest. He shook his head and began to sob. "I'm lost. I'm just like the demon. I'm damned! There's no going back."

"I can save you!" Garvey declared, holding out his hand. "Let me lead you back to salvation!"

William's body began to contort. It bent over and then threw its shoulders up and back as its arms curled up and then extended.

"It's trying to take over!" William yelled haltingly. He was fighting to keep speaking as himself.

William bent over the decapitated body of Father Duncan and hurriedly rifled through the blood-soaked pants pockets. He pulled out the two remaining vials of holy water and tossed them to Jack.

William struggled to say one last word to Jack, "Door!"

Jack immediately knew what William was trying to tell him. He uncorked one vial of holy water and splashed it on the door at the latch. He turned the knob and pulled at the door. It opened. Jack grabbed Clementine's hand and rushed through the door into the smoke-filled hall. He then went back and put his shoulder against the door, as it had begun to close again.

"Hurry, Father!" Jack called after Garvey as he struggled and strained to hold the door open. "That son of a bitch is getting control back and closing the door!"

Garvey nodded and made it out of the room just as the door overpowered Jack and slammed itself shut. It hit the doorframe with such force that it produced a thundering boom down the hall.

*

As the smoke thickened, the three struggled to see in front of them as they ran away from the exorcism room. They finally resorted to feeling the hallway's wall to find the kitchen. Far down the hall, the ceiling was beginning to burn. It was dropping red-hot embers onto the stone floor, creating a shower of fire.

Jack's hand finally found the open archway that led to the kitchen. Then Clementine and Garvey followed Jack in to regroup.

"Well, Father, here are our options," Jack began. "We can't go down the hall because of the fire. And we can't go back that way because of Gray. I'm open to suggestions."

Father Garvey was in a sullen and regretful haze. He looked defeated, having lost his fellow priest and failing to exorcise the demon from William. He nodded at Jack and tried to reassure the Banks—and himself. "We have to have faith, Detective. We are still alive and have God on our side. The Lord will help us, I'm sure of it."

"Well, the Lord certainly didn't help Father Duncan," Jack replied sarcastically. "I'm feeling a little forsaken, Garvey!"

Before Garvey could respond, Clementine stepped in and said, "The Lord helps those who help themselves! Father Garvey, do you know where the dish towels are?"

Garvey looked confused, "Dish towels? This isn't my parish. Father Duncan brought me in to…"

"Never mind!" Clementine interrupted. She quickly began opening cabinet doors and drawers in her search for the towels.

"What's your plan, Clem?" Jack asked as he began helping her search.

Clementine never stopped searching as she explained, "We can't go back towards that room. Our only choice is to go through the fire. We soak the towels in water and put them over our heads to protect them from the embers."

Father Garvey looked apprehensive and asked, "What about the rest of our bodies?

"Better to get a few burns than to burn forever with that demon!" said Clementine.

"I knew I married you for a reason," Jack said as he continued opening drawers. He smiled and added, "And I thought it was for the free health care!"

"I love you, too!" answered Clementine in a snarky tone. She opened a pantry door and saw a stack of folded white towels. "Ah! I found them!"

She grabbed all she could hold and carried them to the sink. "Hurry up! Let's get them soaked. The smoke's getting thicker!"

Jack got the remaining towels and followed his wife to the sink. He threw them all in the pile made by Clementine.

She turned both handles to get maximum pressure and was rewarded with a trickle. "No pressure?" Clementine frustratingly asked.

"They're using the fire hoses upstairs on the fire!" Jack said. "It's draining the water lines. We'll have to make do with what water we can get!"

The Banks soaked as many towels as they thought they needed. Clementine gave a few to Father Garvey and showed him how to hold them above his head.

"Here, Father," explained Clementine, "drape it over your face to keep the smoke out of your lungs. And let it hang in the back to keep the embers off your neck. Slump over as much as you can. The smoke's thinner toward the floor."

When they had affixed the towels, Jack said, "Everybody ready? OK. We'll be moving quick down the hallway. Use the wall as a guide. The hall leads directly to the stairs that go up to the main floor and the outside. Try to keep together as close as you can. And, for God's sake, don't fall! Father, if the Lord's gonna help us, it's now. Any encouraging words you can pass on to him, I wish you would."

"Hush, Jack!" chided Clementine. "The smoke's getting thicker. Let's just go!"

"You're right, Clem. C'mon!" Jack said.

*

The Bankses and Father Garvey took a deep breath and quickly headed out of the kitchen and down the hall to find the stairs, touching the wall with their elbows to keep close to it. The wall was used as a guide for the three. They walked as fast as they could in single file toward their goal—Jack and Clementine in front with Garvey bringing up the rear.

"The smoke's getting thicker!" declared Clementine.

"We must be getting nearer the flames!" Jack yelled with a cough. "Keep going!"

The three pressed on. Now, they were in the thick of the inferno. Red, hot, enflamed embers rained from above them. When they landed on their backs or arms, the cinders quickly burned holes in their clothing and began to sear their skin. All they could do was try to shake them off before the smoldering ashes burned too far into their bodies. As they went forward, the rain of fire intensified.

The fire had been burning the wooden floor above them and into the floor joists. One of them had burned through enough on one end that the joist could no longer support its own weight. It broke from the wall and collapsed through the ceiling in front of the escapees. It made them stop. The end that had broken was on their side of the hall, forming a burning triangle before them. Their choices were to abandon the wall and go under the joist's high point on the other side or jump over the burning end of the joist that was propped up on the stone floor of the church basement.

"Jump over it!" demanded Jack.

"What?" asked a frantic Clementine. "Are you crazy? It'll catch my dress on fire!"

"We'll deal with that on the other side! We're wasting time! We're almost to the stairs!" Jack yelled.

Jack went first. He jumped over the wide joist with ease. Clementine came next. She had to let her towel rest around her neck as she attempted to lift her dress as high as she could to make the jump.

"C'mon, Clem!" yelled Jack.

Clementine backed up a step and leaped over the red-hot joist. Flames licked at her legs, burning them slightly as she passed over the thick burning end of the plank. The hem of her dress caught fire, and she completed the jump. Jack caught her and brought her to the floor, rolling her around and patting out the small flames eating the dress to extinguish them. He was successful at putting out the fires and dragged his wife out of the way so Garvey could make his jump.

"Holy Father!" exclaimed the priest as he went over the burning joist. His first foot cleared the flames. But his trailing foot caught the wood by its heel. Father Garvey tumbled onto the stone floor with the bottom of his left pant leg on fire. He quickly sat up and patted it out.

Garvey looked up towards heaven and asked, "Not enough prayer?"

"Get your ass up, Father!" commanded Jack. "We have to be getting near the end!"

Garvey picked himself up and straightened the cross that hung around his neck. He repositioned the towel over his head and used his elbow as a guide against the wall.

"I'm coming!" answered Garvey.

As they continued, Jack started to notice the smoke was getting slightly thinner. "We must be on the other side of where the fire started. I think I can see further through the smoke."

Then Jack's elbow felt the wall end. Around the corner were the stairs that led up to the street level and the main floor of the church.

The detective smiled and exclaimed, "We're here! Let's get out of this hellhole!"

"No arguments from me!" Clementine agreed. "Let's go!"

They rounded the corner and gazed upon the stairs and their way out, their faces breaking into genuine smiles of relief and salvation. They quickly rushed to the steps. But then, they stopped. The smoke around the stairs began to swirl. The fire behind them began to generate a heavy wind. It caught the swirling wisp, and it started to take form. It was forming into the body of Gray, the demon.

The thing stood before them in a form very different from William's likeness. The creature that manifested was more animal than man. Its furry arms were elongated with hands stretched well below its knees when standing erect. The legs were long, too. The creature seemed to stand on its toes with its knees bent backward, like the back legs of a canine or equine animal. Its bare chest heaved in and out, as if it could not get enough air. The mouth formed an elongated snout, like that of a wolf. Its eyes were entirely black like coal, and its gaze was penetrating. Black shiny fur covered its grinning face.

As Gray closed his black eyes down to a squint, it began to speak.

"Did you think that measly worm could hold me for long?" asked the demon.

Kelly Key

CHAPTER 18

"Are you trying to scare us with this…appearance, Gray?" Jack asked, presenting a brave front by degrading the demon's transformation.

"It suits me for this occasion, Detective," answered the demon. "And I believe it's working. Isn't that right, Clementine?"

"Go to hell!" yelled Clementine defiantly.

"I find that amusing," said the demon to Clementine. "Yes, of you three, you're the most frightened. I can feel your fear increasing. Perhaps I should possess you next and feed off you till the end of time."

Father Garvey laid his hand on Clementine's shoulder and declared to the demon, "I won't allow that. To get to her, you'll have to come through me!"

217

"You guessed my plan!" taunted the beast.

The priest turned Clementine around to face him. He said, reassuringly, "This isn't real, my child. The demon is an ethereal spirit, not this monster it presents. It's a trick…all an illusion. Calm yourself."

"Yes," Gray interrupted. "Let us see how calm she can be!"

The monstrous apparition charged at Clementine. Jack jumped in front of the demon, holding his last bottle of holy water. He opened it and splashed Gray's black eyes. The demon shut its eyes in reaction to the splash. The eyelids hissed and steamed. This made the demon stop, step back, and stagger as it rubbed its eyes to clear them.

Taking advantage of the weakened creature, Jack lowered his shoulder and ran into the thing's midsection. It stumbled backward and fell to the basement floor with the detective on top of it. Jack rose to a kneeling position and began punching the demon's snout repeatedly.

Jack yelled each word with a corresponding blow, "Leave…my…wife…alone!"

Gray then opened its eyes and grinned. The holy water had momentarily incapacitated it. The demon had recovered and was ready to do battle. It grabbed Jack's punching arm and pulled him off its chest. It tossed the detective toward Clementine and Father Garvey, knocking both down to the floor.

The demon rose and stood above the three, all lying on their backs. They held onto each other, each helping the other to stand.

"Pitiful weaklings," it taunted. "You should beg me to release your souls from those frail and fragile bodies. For example, behold!"

The creature grabbed Father Garvey by his left arm and snapped the two bones below the elbow. The priest screamed in agony and fell to his knees. With his good hand, Garvey cradled the broken limb, which had a noticeable sag between his hand and the elbow.

With all the attention on the fallen priest, the demon took advantage and grabbed Clementine away from Jack. The monster dragged her across the floor toward the inferno that was the church hallway. The floor above them had given way and collapsed through the ceiling to the basement, leaving a massive pile of burning debris of joists and red-hot church pews.

"Jack!" Clementine screamed. She struggled to pry her arm out of Gray's grip.

"You spoke of hell earlier, Clem," it began. "You have no idea the levels of pain and suffering in that place. But perhaps I can give you a sample!"

As it continued to drag Clementine toward the flaming debris, Jack was desperately looking for a weapon, anything to make the thing release his wife. He instinctively pulled his pistol out of his shoulder holster. Then, he remembered how the bullets sailed through the demon at his mother-in-law's apartment building. Besides, he thought he might hit Clementine.

"Shit! Father, you got any more holy water?" Jack asked, reholstering his gun.

"No," Garvey uttered, still in pain.

"Shit!" exclaimed Jack. He ran down the fiery hall to save Clementine. He jumped into the air to land on Gray's immense shoulder. With both of his hands, he tried to pry Clementine free from the hand of the demon. Gray was not phased. It continued dragging the resisting Clementine to the rising flames.

Then, from behind the demon, Father Garvey started to speak. With his left arm hanging limp by his side, he held up his Saint Benedict medal with his right hand and began chanting:

"Crux sacra sit mihi lux, non draco sit mihi dux: vade retro satana!

"Crux sacra sit mihi lux, non draco sit mihi dux: vade retro satana!

"Crux sacra sit mihi lux, non draco sit mihi dux: vade retro satana!"

The priest was reciting an exorcism prayer that meant, "May the Holy Cross be my light, may the dragon never be my guide: Begone, Satan!"

The demon stopped and looked at Father Garvey. Its body formed a darkened silhouette against the flames behind it. As it shook its wolfen-like head, it responded, "Save your breath…Padre! You have no idea how many times over the millennia those incantations have been spat at me."

"They're not incantations, devil!" protested Garvey. "They're prayers to send you back to hell!"

The demon then nodded at the priest and said, "Well, well, Father. If you're trying to send me to hell, I'm taking these two with me!"

With his free hand, Gray reached up to its hairy shoulder and wrapped its enormous hand around Jack's neck. The beast now held both Clementine and

Jack up in the air in front of the priest as if displaying its catches of the day. While smiling, the demon turned back towards the fire, intending to burn Clementine and Jack alive.

Jack pulled at the monster's grip with both of his hands. The grip was so tight on his neck that he could barely breathe. He looked over at Clementine and saw that she was struggling as well. Both began to feel the heat being generated from the flames.

Jack heard Father Garvey behind him, continuing with his prayers. He wondered if prayer was the only weapon they had left.

The demon took pleasure in playing with its prey. It held Jack and Clementine over the flames and then pulled them back. Like a cat playing with a wounded mouse, it was teasing them with their fate.

As the flames began to lick at Jack and Clementine, he saw a figure on the other side of the fire. It was William. He had made it out of the room where Gray had imprisoned him. The detective thought that the demon might have turned its attention from William to combat the priest, Clementine, and himself. Jack saw he had a look of determination on his face—a look of defiance.

"William?" Jack said hoarsely. He wasn't sure the accountant could hear him over the roar of the flames and Father Garvey's prayers. "William, can you take it back into you?"

William nodded. He raised his arms above his head and shouted, "Demon! Join with me! You are with me and I with you!" William paused for a moment.

He appeared to be unsure of himself about what to do next. After inhaling deeply, he nodded again and shouted, "I SUMMON YOU! I COMMAND IT!"

The orders stopped Gray from going forward. It raised Clementine above his head to throw her into the flames that were the remains of the ceiling and joists that had crashed down from above. As it smiled and pulled its arm back for the throw, Clementine fell from its grip and down to the floor.

On the demon's other hand, Jack slipped through the monster's grip. It was as if there was nothing there to hold him anymore. He fell to the floor beside Clementine. Both of them scrambled away from the demon toward Father Garvey.

"C'mon, Clemmie! Run like hell!" Jack yelled. He picked her up from her crawling position and pushed her ahead of him.

The demon bent down and reached for Jack. Its hand passed through Jack's torso.

Jack saw the hand go through him. He never broke stride and kept running towards Garvey. Both he and Clementine reached the priest at the same time. They turned to look back at the demon.

"What's happening?" asked a confused Gray out loud to William. "You don't command me! I command you!"

"DEMON, YOU HAVE BONDED WITH ME! COME!" William demanded.

Gray looked at its hands as they faded away. Its arms were next. They seemed to be fading away from reality. As its head began to turn to mist, the demon let out a defiant, shrieking scream that started to fade with Gray as it disappeared. The fire's breeze blew away the fog that was left of the demon's apparition. The scream then continued from within William.

Father Garvey broke out in a look of wonder. "Did my prayers finally work? Is it gone?"

"Yes and no, Father," said Jack. "You had a little help. William took it back."

Across the flames, William doubled over, screaming in pain. His body began to contort again.

"No!" William screamed. "I won't let you out! You're my prisoner now!"

Jack looked up at the ever-growing hole in the ceiling to see that the entire church above them was on fire. He knew it wouldn't be long before the whole structure would collapse into itself.

"We gotta get out of here," said Jack.

"No arguments here," agreed Clementine. She helped Father Garvey cradle his broken arm and led him toward the stairs to the street. "C'mon, Father."

"William!" Jack yelled across the flames. "Stay put! I'm coming to help you out!"

"No, Detective! There is only one way out for us!" William uttered through the pain. "I don't know how long I can hold him inside my body. So, I'll have to do this quickly."

"What?" Jack asked. "What are you talking about, William? "If I go, it goes with me!" William explained. With that, William raised his hands and walked into the fire.

"What the hell?" Jack yelled, shocked at William's march into the flames. "William! Don't!"

The flames grabbed William's dark wool pants first. Then, they quickly climbed up his torso until William was fully engulfed. Now, a fireball that was dancing in the flames as the demon contorted William's body in an attempt to escape. The shrill screams were either coming from the man or the demon.

"Ah, William!" Jack screamed. He could no longer bear to see the man he had promised to save die in such an excruciating fashion. The detective pulled his pistol from his shoulder holster and, with both hands, aimed at the struggling fireball that William had become.

The first shot hit William square in the middle of William's back. That stopped the dance of death. William turned to face Jack. The detective thought he could see William smile at him. He was getting what he had begged for since his possession began.

The second shot struck William's head just below his left eye. William wavered after the bullet hit and then collapsed into the flames.

The detective lowered his weapon and shook his head. He thought about how much he'd tried to help that poor soul, only to take him down to relieve his pain ultimately. He felt an overwhelming sense of failure.

"I'm sorry, William," Jack uttered. "I hope you can find peace someday…"

224

More of the ceiling collapsed on top of the pyre where William's body had fallen. Jack backed away from the flames and turned to climb the steps that led to the street above. He joined Father Garvey and Clementine on the other side of the street from the church. They had moved there for safety from the collapsing stones.

"We heard gunshots, Jack," Clementine said desperately. "What happened?"

Jack smiled at Clementine and cupped her face with one hand. He then looked at Father Garvey.

"Forgive me, Father, for I have sinned," Jack said. "I killed William to put him out of his misery. He had thrown himself into the fire to keep Gray with him. Know that it was a killing of mercy, not malice."

"A sin is a sin, my child," Father Garvey answered. "But I'm sure in your line of work, you have and will run into the conundrum of taking lives. I'd absolve you if you were Catholic."

"After all this, I might be!" Jack replied. "My beliefs have certainly been altered."

"I can't say the same thing for Mr. Arbogast," Garvey said. "He died with that mortal sin still upon him. I feel that we failed for not saving his soul."

"But we didn't fail," Clementine explained. "William died a hero's death. He kept that demon and took it with him. I hope he's saved a lot of souls from it."

"The big question is, can he keep hold of it?" said Jack.

"Holding on to an evil spirit is the saints' work. He'll be a blessed man if he can do it."

Jack looked over to the church, which was collapsing into a fiery inferno. "I guess this case is closed."

"What are you gonna tell the Chief?" asked Clementine.

Jack paused to think before answering his wife. He hadn't thought far enough ahead as to what report this series of events would be. He worked out a scenario inside his head before speaking.

"The truth," Jack began as he shrugged his shoulders. "I'm putting in my report that William found the true murderer and killed him. They fell into the fire together and were burned up. That way, I don't have to tell who the true killer is because I didn't find out."

"A lie of omission?" Clementine said with a suspicious side-eye.

"Corpus Delicti," said Jack.

"Where's the body…" Father Garvey said with a smile of recognition, translating the Latin and nodding his head.

Jack smiled at the priest, "Thanks, Father. No body, no crime."

"So, you basically botched the case to protect William? You think the Chief will believe it?" asked Clementine.

"Hey, not every case is solved to the law's satisfaction. And the Chief's so tired of this case that he'll believe anything to get rid of it," Jack said. He smiled at a relieved Clementine and threw his arm around her. "C'mon. Let's get the Father fixed up and go home!"

*

The three walked away from the burning church, leaving William's body at the bottom of the rubble to be wholly consumed and cremated. The flame was finally extinguished in a few hours. But it smoldered for weeks. Smoke and steam danced in the breeze and rose from the blackened ashes to the sky, as there was no longer a roof to stop them.

Or was it a mist that rose from the ashes?

THE END

ABOUT THE AUTHOR

Kelly Key started late with his writing career. His younger years were spent working in the music industry in Nashville, Tennessee. He wrote his first novel, *Brimstone-A Myth of Terror in the Old West*, in his forties. Making up for lost time, other novels followed in quick succession. His next novel was a romantic comedy titled *Wedding Secrets*. A murder mystery followed this: *You Can't Tell*. Kelly then wrote his popular Blackburn Witches Trilogy: *Bloody Bones, Bloody Bones: Rise of the Witch Twins*, and finally, *Bloody Bones: The Warlock War*. Kelly also wrote a Gothic novel about a family in Tennessee: *Decoration Day*. *The Alibi* is Kelly's eighth novel.

All of Kelly Key's books can be found on his website: https://kellykeybooks.com/